Pr~~i~~ ~~vok~~ing the GRUMPY CEO

Jax KANE
WHERE DANGER MEETS DESIRE

© Copyright Jax Kane 2025 - **All rights reserved.**

The content within this book may not be reproduced, duplicated or transmitted without direct written permission from the author or the publisher.

Under no circumstances will any blame or legal responsibility be held against the publisher, or author, for any damages, reparation, or monetary loss due to the information contained within this book. Either directly or indirectly. You are responsible for your own choices, actions, and results.

Legal Notice:

This book is copyright protected. This book is only for personal use. You cannot amend, distribute, sell, use, quote or paraphrase any part, of the content within this book, without the consent of the author or publisher.

Disclaimer Notice:

Please note the information contained within this document is for educational and entertainment purposes only. All effort has been expended to present accurate, up-to-date, and reliable, complete information. No warranties of any kind are declared or implied. Readers acknowledge that the author is not engaging in the rendering of legal, financial, medical or professional advice. The content within this book has been derived from various sources. Please consult a licensed professional before attempting any techniques outlined in this book.

By reading this document, the reader agrees that under no circumstances is the author responsible for any losses, direct or indirect, which are incurred as a result of the use of the information contained within this document, including, but not limited to, — errors, omissions, or inaccuracies.

Contents

1. The Unwanted Assignment — 1
2. Reluctant Alliance — 9
3. Clashing Wills — 15
4. The First Layer — 22
5. Breaking Down Walls — 30
6. Uncovering Secrets — 39
7. Dangerous Liaisons — 49
8. The Reckoning — 56
9. Trust Issues — 63
10. Emotions Unraveled — 71
11. Under Attack — 77
12. The Unseen Enemy — 85
13. Reckless Decisions — 100
14. The Rescue Mission — 105
15. Breaking Point — 112
16. Healing and Recovery — 118
17. Final Confrontation — 128
18. Love in the Line of Fire — 134

19. Promise of a New Beginning	142
Want to join Jax' Inner Circle?	148
A Few Final Words From Jax	149

Chapter 1
The Unwanted Assignment
Blake Carter

I had taken my fair share of unpleasant assignments, but this one might take the cake.

Standing in the back of the opulent event hall, arms crossed, I surveyed the chaos in front of me. Spotlights flashed, cameras clicked, and journalists barked out questions. The product pre-launch for Avery Lane's cybersecurity software, Vanguard, was a media circus. And I hated media circuses.

I didn't do high-profile. I didn't do spoiled billionaires who thought they were untouchable. And I sure as hell didn't do corporate politics.

But here I was, babysitting Avery Lane.

The corporate board had called me in after several threats had been made against the CEO, threats she had reportedly ignored. With the upcoming release of her latest software, the intimidation had escalated. I had been reluctant, but a paycheck was a paycheck. Sierra Bravo Security didn't turn down work.

Avery herself was another problem. I had been warned she wouldn't be cooperative, that she had resisted the board's insistence on hiring a bodyguard. Ha! I'd gotten more cooperation from two-year-olds.

Right now, I was scanning the room, looking for anything suspicious. Security was tight, but not tight enough in my opinion. I'd already noted weaknesses in the event layout.

Warren Merrick, Mr. Chairman of the Board himself, glanced my way. He raised his eyebrows and nodded slightly. No clue what that meant. A comment on my lack of formal attire at this swanky event or simply acknowledging that I'm here doing my job? He plays everything like he either has a royal flush or he's totally bluffing, and I can't tell which. I just don't trust him, but I only met him when he hired me. Maybe it's just my prejudice against these corporate types showing.

Then I saw her.

Avery Lane moved through the crowd like she owned the place. Probably because she did. Tall, poised, and commanding, she wore a sleek black dress that screamed power and sophistication. Her platinum blond hair was in a perfect updo. Gold sparkled from her earlobes and neck. Her dark eyes were sharp, but there was something else in them, something more fragile than she'd like anyone to see.

I was good at reading people. Had to be in my job. Despite her polish and confidence, she was carrying more weight on her shoulders than she let on. Might just be an occupational hazard of having the corner office.

My first instinct? Ignore it. I was just here to keep her alive.

Then the lights flickered.

It was brief, just a few seconds. but enough to send a murmur through the crowd. The massive digital screens displaying her company's branding glitched, static filling them before blinking back to life.

My spine stiffened.

To most, it was probably just a power surge. To me, it was a sign that something maybe wasn't right. I never assume something is a coincidence. To me, everything is an act of malice until proven otherwise.

I pushed through the crowd, heading straight for Avery. She was already turning toward one of her team members, no doubt asking about the malfunction. I didn't wait for an introduction.

"We need to talk." I said, just as a gambit to get her moving.

Avery turned, her gaze locking onto mine. "Excuse me?"

"Blake Carter. I'm your security."

Her expression hardened. "I don't need security."

"That's not your call."

She let out a slow breath, eyes widening "I appreciate the board's concern, but I have my own security team."

I smirked. "You sure? Because from where I'm standing, your security just let a potential breach happen right under their noses."

Her lips parted slightly. She glanced at the screens, then squared her shoulders.

"It was nothing. A minor technical issue. Happens all the time."

I leaned in. "Maybe. Or maybe it was a test run."

For a moment, something flickered in her eyes, uncertainty, maybe. But just as quickly, it was gone.

"I don't have time for paranoia." She turned away. "Enjoy the party, *Mr.* Carter."

I clenched my jaw. This was going to be a freakin long assignment.

Before I could follow her, a commotion near the stage caught my attention. One of the event staff was arguing with one of her security guards, waving a piece of paper. I moved toward them.

"What's going on?" I demanded.

The staff member looked panicked. "This was found backstage."

I took the paper. Three words were scrawled in red ink:

WATCH YOUR BACK.

And beneath it, Avery's name.

My gut tightened. Whatever this was, it wasn't just a scare tactic. This was a warning and that meant finding Miss Who Ignores Me and getting her out of here.

I turned on my heel and spotted her talking to some event person. I marched straight over to her, taking her forearm.

"What?" she started as I began leading her out of the room.

"We are leaving." I stated.

I led Avery toward the nearest exit, keeping my hand around her forearm. I wasn't about to take chances. Whoever had left that note had gotten close enough to deliver a message, and that meant they could be planning something, certainly watching.

Avery was tense under my touch. "I don't see why we need to leave in such a hurry. This is my event. People expect ..." she insisted.

I didn't have time for arguments. "It's not up for debate." I interrupted.

"Of course not." Her tone was laced with frustration.

I let out a short breath. "This isn't about your independence. It's about keeping you alive."

We reached the side doors. "We need her car brought around. Now." I told the guard standing there.

The guard hesitated. "Ma'am, your driver is still parked at the south entrance—"

I cut him off. "I'm giving the orders. Tell him to move. Five minutes."

Avery crossed her arms. "You always this bossy?"

"Only when someone's life is on the line." I faced her. "Someone wants to hurt you."

I was going to repeat my mantra until it sunk into her pretty head that I wasn't here as window dressing. You don't pay what Sierra Bravo charges unless you are sincerely worried and want the best. That is what her board did. I was not going to sit back while my charge got killed because she was too stupid to understand reality. No one had ever died in our charge. I intended to keep it that way.

"I just … I don't understand. Who would want to hurt me?"

"That's what I intend to find out," I said. "But I need you to work with me."

She held my gaze before nodding. "Fine."

Our moment of agreement was short-lived.

Just as the guard finished radioing in for her car, a loud *crack* split through the night air.

Gunfire.

I didn't think. I reacted. I grabbed Avery, pulling her down behind a parked van as another shot rang out, shattering the glass of a nearby lamppost. People screamed, ducking for cover.

"Stay low," I ordered.

Avery's breath was fast, her eyes wide. "Someone's shooting at me?"

I pulled my gun. "No kidding."

More gunfire. We needed to move.

"Come on," I said, gripping her wrist as I drug her toward the parking area. "We need to get out of here. Now."

Avery didn't argue.

She ran beside me. I kept myself between her and the direction of the shots. Whoever was out there wasn't just trying to scare her. They were trying to kill her.

And I wasn't about to let that happen.

I pulled Avery behind a thick concrete pillar, pressing her against it to keep her out of the line of fire. My mind worked fast, cataloging the angles, the sound of the gunfire, and the likely position of the shooter. A professional would have taken her out with the first shot. This wasn't about precision. It was about panic. So far.

Avery's breath was uneven, but she held herself together, gripping my arm as if trying to ground herself. "Do you see them?"

"Not yet," I said quietly, scanning the rooftop across the street. "But they're out there."

Security personnel scrambled, shouting into their radios. I knew how this would play out. They were too slow, too reactive. The shooter could tell their positions by their panicked voices. This would be the last time I didn't have my own team on the ground. I needed to get Avery out of here before the shooter adjusted their approach.

"We're moving," I said, gripping her wrist again.

Avery dug in her heels. "We can't just—"

I didn't give her time to argue. I moved, keeping her low as we sprinted between parked vehicles. Another shot rang out, hitting the hood of a nearby sedan. The shooter was trying to predict our movement. Bad luck for them. I had spent years outmaneuvering people with far better aim. We reached the loading dock, shielded from view. I pressed her against the metal siding, eyes darting to the exit route. The car would be there in seconds.

"You okay?" I asked.

Avery nodded, though her face was pale. "I'm fine."

I almost believed her. Though 'fine' invariably meant anything but.

The SUV pulled up, tires screeching. I yanked open the door and pushed Avery inside before sliding in next to her. "Drive!"

That was another thing on my list. Either I would be driving, or it would be a driver from Sierra Bravo. I doubted her driver had taken any defensive evasion training.

The vehicle peeled away from the curb, leaving the chaos behind.

Avery exhaled, pressing a hand to her forehead. "Is this what my life is going to be now?"

I glanced at her. "Until we figure out who's after you? Probably."

She let out a slow breath. "Great."

I smirked despite myself. She had done a fast recovery for having been shot at and dashing through a parking garage. "You'll get used to it."

Her sharp gaze snapped to me. "I really hope I don't have to."

I didn't respond. I just kept my eyes on the road, knowing this was only the beginning.

Silence filled the car for a long moment, the only sound the hum of the engine and the distant sirens from the event behind us. Avery sat rigid in her seat, staring out the window as if replaying the last few minutes in her head. I had seen that look before, the moment when adrenaline faded, and reality set in.

She wasn't just a billionaire CEO anymore.

She was a target.

I reached for my phone, dialing a secure number. "Sierra, it's Carter. I need a security sweep at Lane's residence. Full lockdown."

Avery's head whipped toward me. "Excuse me? You don't get to make that decision for me."

I kept my eyes forward. "You want to argue, or you want to live?"

She folded her arms, her frustration clear, but she didn't argue.

Smart woman.

The moment we arrived at her penthouse, the place would be secured, exits reinforced, surveillance systems checked. I wasn't about to let her walk into another potential death trap.

Avery exhaled sharply. "I suppose this is where you tell me I'm under house arrest?"

"Close," I said. "You're under *my* watch."

She rolled her eyes but didn't protest.

I leaned back, watching her for a moment. The fear was still there, just beneath the surface. But so was something else.

Determination.

Good.

She was going to need it.

Chapter 2
Reluctant Alliance

Avery Lane

I had built an empire on control. I had been forced to prove over and over that a woman could master tech, create cutting edge software and run a profitable company without relying on a man to help her. There were plenty of men in the company but if I ever showed the least bit of weakness, the media, the competition, everyone would have a feeding frenzy. I had to maintain my image. Losing control was not an option.

Yet here I was, pacing the sleek boardroom of Lane Technologies, while a hired bodyguard Blake Carter, sat in one of the chairs like he had every right to be there. My God. He was dressed in a worn brown leather jacket, a black t-shirt and blue jeans. He should have been delivering pizza in here or, more likely, hanging out at a biker bar instead of coming in like a hero-wanna-be that is going to make me look like I am cowering behind a man.

"This is ridiculous," I snapped. "I have my own security team. They're trained, competent, and they've kept me safe for years."

Blake leaned back, arms crossed. "Yeah? And yet, someone left you a death threat and took a shot at you last night. But sure, your security team's got it covered."

I gritted my teeth, refusing the bait. "That was an isolated incident."

Blake arched a brow. "You sure about that?"

I turned to the corporate board, frustration barely contained. "I appreciate your concern, but this is overkill. We don't even know if these threats are credible."

"An armed attack at a public event is pretty damn credible," Blake muttered.

Board chair Merrick cleared his throat. "Avery, this isn't a debate. The board has voted, and Blake stays. We're not taking risks. Particularly with the imminent launch of Vanguard."

My stomach tightened. I hated being backed into a corner.

I straightened. "Fine. But let's get one thing clear. I run this company and my life." I turned to glare at Blake. "Not him."

Blake smirked. "Trust me, sweetheart, I don't want to run your company. Just keep you alive."

I clenched my jaw, barely containing an eye roll. I had broken myself of that habit years ago and Mr. Attitude wasn't going to push me into it now. This was going to be a long day.

I just had no idea how bad it would be. The forced proximity started immediately.

Blake shadowed me everywhere. He lounged in my office. He followed me to meetings. When I went out to talk to my assistant, there he was. When I ducked into the CFO's office, he was close enough to overhear.

"Do you have to hover?" I snapped.

Blake didn't even blink. "Yes."

I exhaled sharply. "This isn't a war zone."

"Until I know who's after you, you're a target and I'll treat this anyway I like."

I huffed and stalked toward the conference room for my next meeting. If he was going to play shadow, fine. I'd pretend he didn't exist.

Easier said than done.

The meeting was in full swing when the lights flickered. The Marketing VP barely paused in his presentation, but when static cut through his slides, I felt it. Was it a warning like last night? No. That was just me catching Blake's paranoia.

Blake, seated against the back wall, shifted slightly. The VP pressed on, refusing to let minor technical hiccups rattle him. "As you can see, our earnings are projected to surpass last year's by eighteen percent. With the Vanguard launch—"

The room plunged into darkness. Muffled gasps filled the space. Then, emergency lighting flickered on. My fingers tightened around the tabletop next to the built-in keyboard. Blake was already standing away from the wall.

"Stay here," he ordered.

I barely had time to get annoyed before he was at the door, barking orders. I hadn't planned on going anywhere. Minutes passed before the main power returned.

Blake returned, unreadable. "Security is sweeping the building. No explanation yet."

I met his gaze. "You think it was intentional?" and that comment raised some muttering around the table.

"Wouldn't rule it out."

A cold knot formed in my stomach. The meeting wrapped up, but my mind wasn't on the numbers anymore. Blake stood near the entrance, scanning the hallway. Then he stiffened. I followed his line of sight, but whoever he had been looking at was gone or had never been there. Blake swore under his breath.

"What is it?" I asked not liking being kept in the dark.

He hesitated, then shook his head. "Nothing. Not yet."

But the tension in his shoulders told me otherwise and that irritated me more. He was not the boss here. He had no right keeping things from me.

The next morning, Blake was waiting at the parking lot elevator.

"This is unnecessary," I said as I passed him knowing full well he could hear me.

Blake fell into step beside me. "That's what you said yesterday."

I shot him a glare. "You're enjoying this, aren't you?"

"Lady, I could think of a hundred places I'd rather be."

My assistant, Danielle, looked at Blake with wide eyes as I left the elevator. "Should I schedule additional security?"

"No," I snapped before Blake could speak.

That was the absolute last thing I needed: more albatrosses around my neck. I was certain someone in the media would be noticing Carter soon enough and start making inquiries. Just what I didn't need in the face of launching Vanguard.

Blake shrugged. "Your call."

Inside my office, I turned away from the floor to ceiling windows with their view of the city. "Are you *seriously* planning to follow me *everywhere*?"

Blake crossed his arms. "That's the job."

I let out a slow breath. "Fine. Just ... stay out of my way."

Blake smirked. "I'll do my best."

I doubted that.

The morning passed in the usual blur of meetings, but I couldn't ignore Blake's presence. It was unnerving. Not just because he was always there, but because...Because I was getting used to it. I caught myself glancing at him. Not just out of irritation, but curiosity. He was a mystery—one moment dead serious, the next effortlessly sarcastic. His presence was both aggravating and, strangely, reassuring. Which made no sense. I didn't need reassurance. I was still convincing myself of that when the power flickered, *again*. This time, I couldn't simply dismiss it.

Blake was on his feet before I could react.

"Someone's testing your systems," he growled.

My pulse quickened. "How do you know?"

"I've seen this before." He pulled out his phone revealing a shoulder holster. "We need a security lockdown. Now." he told someone.

I had spent years fortifying my company against cyber threats and corporate espionage. It had been the impetus behind Vanguard. But this, this was different. This was *personal*. For the first time, I realized this might be serious. I wasn't just fighting for my company anymore. I was fighting for my life.

That night, Blake insisted on staying close.

I sighed as we stepped into my penthouse. "You *really* think someone is coming for me tonight?"

It was almost a whine. I really wanted him out of there and to just relax. My brain had focused on a lovely glass of wine in a hot bath.

Blake locked the door behind us. "I think someone already has."

That put a whole different frame around it. I turned toward my bedroom, but his voice stopped me.

"Avery."

I glanced back.

His expression was unreadable. "Get some sleep."

I nodded stiffly and shut the door. But sleep never came. Because for the first time, I felt truly unsafe. And the only person standing between me and whoever wanted to get to me... was Blake Carter. The stranger on the far side of the bedroom door in my apartment.

Chapter 3
Clashing Wills
Blake Carter

I believed in control. The more, the better. Without it, people got hurt.

Which was why I was currently making Avery Lane's life as difficult as humanly possible.

"You're overreacting," she snapped, arms crossed as she stood in the doorway of her office. "This level of security is unnecessary."

I barely glanced at her as I finished inspecting the lock on her window. "You almost got shot two days ago, Lane. Humor me."

She let out an exasperated sigh. "I already have security."

"Then fire them."

She gaped at me. "Excuse me?"

I finally turned, arms crossed over my chest. "Your security team missed a death threat, let someone slip into your building, and didn't notice the guy casing your office yesterday. So yeah, if I were you, I'd fire them."

Her jaw clenched. "This is my company, Carter. I decide who protects me."

I smirked. "And yet, here I am."

Her glare could have burned through steel. I knew I was rubbing it in. I had seen that her board overruling her objections in hiring me had almost made her blow a gasket. I didn't know precisely why unless she was just used to controlling everything. Can't control life, sweetheart, particularly when someone makes it their business to come after you.

I didn't care what her issues were. I had a job to do, and I would not fail.

By noon, I'd tripled the security detail and overhauled her schedule, cutting out unnecessary stops and ensuring she was never alone in unsecured areas. I assigned two additional guards to her penthouse and reviewed all building access logs.

It pissed her off. Which was fine. I wasn't here to make her happy, only keep her alive.

"What do you mean I can't take my usual route to the office?" Avery demanded as she stared at her assistant, Danielle.

Danielle shifted uncomfortably. "Mr. Carter suggested an alternate path."

Avery spun to face me. "Suggested?"

I leaned against her desk. "Your *usual* route is predictable. That's a problem. We're going to fix that by making it random."

Her nails tapped against the polished wood. "You don't get to dictate how I live my life."

I shrugged. "Actually, I do."

Her nostrils flared. "You're unbelievable."

I grinned. "You're welcome."

While Avery fumed, I walked her penthouse one last time, checking for weaknesses. I found three.

The fire escape latch was loose. It was an easy access point for anyone determined enough. The security system had a delay between activation and lockout. Definitely enough time for a skilled intruder to slip through. And the front desk guards weren't paying close enough attention.

Sloppy.

I fixed the latch myself, called the building's security firm about the delay, and had a firm word with the guards. By the time I was done, I felt marginally better. Avery still didn't appreciate it.

"You act like I live in a war zone," she muttered when I returned.

I met her gaze. "Right now, you do."

Something flickered in her expression, something almost vulnerable, but it vanished as quickly as it appeared.

She huffed. "You're impossible."

"Again," I said, smirking. "You're welcome."

Despite the tension, I couldn't ignore the fact that Avery intrigued me. I'd worked for CEOs before, powerful men and women who barked orders and demanded obedience. But Avery wasn't like them. She was sharp, controlled, but beneath the icy exterior, I sensed something else. Loneliness. I didn't know why it bothered me. I wasn't here to figure her out. But that didn't stop me from wondering.

The argument over security and driving routes lasted on and off all day. By the time she finally relented, it was late evening. I walked her to her car, scanning the lot as we approached.

Avery sighed. "I don't need an escort."

I just ignored her. It seemed that would be her constant mantra. I checked her vehicle briefly. Nothing looked off. Still, I couldn't shake the feeling that something was wrong. Maybe because nothing had happened for most of the day.

Avery slid into the driver's seat and started the engine. My gut instinctively clenched. Something wasn't right. Then her car lurched forward, wild, uncontrolled. Avery gasped, hands gripping the wheel.

"Brake!" I yelled.

"I am!" she shouted.

The car didn't stop. It accelerated. Straight toward the wall.

I was already moving. I sprinted alongside the car as it shot forward, heart hammering in my chest. I had seconds, maybe less, before Avery crashed. My body moved on instinct. I lunged for the door handle, yanking it open as she struggled to regain control.

Avery's foot was slamming repetitively on the brake, her hands gripping the wheel in a white-knuckled hold. "It's not stopping!"

I dove across her, my hand closing around the gear shift. With a forceful jerk, I slammed it into neutral. The car let out a sickening screech as the engine fought against the sudden shift, but the acceleration slowed. Tires squealed as Avery finally swerved away from the looming concrete wall, the car shuddering to a stop a few feet away.

For a long second, neither of us moved.

Then Avery let out a shaky breath. "What the hell just happened?"

I didn't answer. I was busy scanning the dashboard, the pedals, the undercarriage. My gut churned as I spotted the culprit. Someone had tampered with the accelerator.

"This wasn't an accident," I swore.

Avery turned sharply. "What do you mean?"

I straightened, jaw tight. "Someone rigged your car."

Avery blinked, her breath still uneven. "You're saying someone tried to—"

"Kill you?" I finished. "Yeah."

Her expression wavered between shock and anger. "That's insane."

I exhaled, getting tired of this same old fight. "Is it?" I gestured to the dashboard. "Someone messed with your acceleration. This wasn't bad wiring or a glitch. Someone wanted you dead."

She ran a hand across her hair, visibly trying to steady herself. "Who?"

"That's what I intend to find out."

I called into Sierra Bravo. Within thirty minutes, a technician confirmed my suspicion.

"The wiring under the accelerator was clipped and rigged to jam," the tech said, shaking his head. "This wasn't amateur work. Whoever did this knew what they were doing."

Avery stood rigid beside me, her arms crossed so tightly it looked like she was holding herself together. But I saw through it. I saw the way her fingers trembled slightly, the way she kept swallowing hard. For once, she had no argument.

I turned to her. "Do you believe me now?"

Her jaw clenched, but she nodded. Good. Because this had just escalated.

Back at her penthouse, I reinforced my security measures. I doubled the guard rotation, added a secondary surveillance sweep, and installed proximity alarms on her doors.

Avery watched; arms still crossed. "So, this is my life now?"

I met her gaze. "Until we find out who's after you? Yeah."

She exhaled, her shoulders dropping slightly. "Great."

I studied her for a beat. "You okay?"

She looked away. "I'm fine."

Liar. Fine always meant anything but.

I didn't push. I knew that look, the forced bravado, the mask that kept people from seeing the cracks underneath. I'd worn it myself. Still, the fact that it bothered me meant I was getting too close. I needed to keep my focus I needed to remember why I was here. Shore up my granite boundaries.

But as I watched Avery move stiffly toward the window, her reflection flickering in the glass, I couldn't shake the thought: Who the hell wanted her dead? And how far would they go to make it happen?

I didn't sleep that night. I spent the next few hours going over every possible angle. Someone had sabotaged Avery's car. Someone had bypassed security, gotten close enough to tamper with it, and had the skill to make it look like an accident.

It wasn't just a random attack. This was personal.

At dawn, I used her kitchen to make coffee. I poured myself a cup and checked the perimeter again. The guards were in position, the surveillance system was live, and the penthouse was secure.

For now.

Avery walked in, still dressed in sleepwear—loose joggers and a fitted tank top. She stopped short when she saw me, her expression wary.

"You don't sleep?" she asked.

I sipped my coffee. "Not when I'm protecting someone."

She rubbed her temples. "This is insane."

"No argument there." I smiled slightly. 'Insane' seemed to be one of her favorite words.

She exhaled, dropping onto the couch. "I just... I don't get it. Why would someone want me dead?"

I watched her carefully. "You tell me."

She scoffed. "I don't exactly have a list of enemies."

"Everyone has enemies."

Avery hesitated. Then, quietly, "I don't know who I can trust."

That was the first honest thing she'd said.

I sat across from her. "Then start with me."

Her gaze flickered to mine, searching for something. After a long moment, she nodded. It wasn't much but it was a start.

Later that morning, Avery insisted on going to work. I didn't argue—I just made damn sure she wasn't alone. I drove. As we stepped into the office lobby, my eyes scanned the crowd. Employees moved through security checkpoints, badges flashing under scanners. I clocked each one, looking for anomalies.

Then I saw one.

A man in a dark suit, lingering too long by the elevators. His stance was too stiff, his gaze too focused. My instincts flared and I moved. The man turned, disappearing into the crowd. I cursed under my breath. Whoever he was, he didn't belong. And that meant only one thing. The threat was closer than we thought.

Chapter 4
The First Layer
Avery Lane

I had never let anyone get too close. I had learned early on that trust was a liability, that the more people knew about me, the more power they had over me. I had chosen the streets over mom's handsy boyfriends, living alone over domineering boyfriends, building my own company when others stole my ideas. Trusting only myself was a lesson I had taken to heart, one that had shaped every decision I had made.

Which was why having Blake Carter in my space, constantly watching, constantly assessing, was starting to wear me down. I felt like I was on guard every second. I was never alone.

"You don't like this," Blake observed, his voice even.

I sat stiffly on the couch in my penthouse, watching as he flipped through files on his tablet, cross-referencing details of my life. My entire world was being dissected in front of me by a stranger. It was simultaneously irritating and nauseating.

"I don't like invasions of privacy," I corrected.

Blake didn't look up. "This is necessary. Someone's trying to kill you. That makes digging into your past critical."

I folded my arms. "I don't see how my childhood or my personal life are relevant."

Blake glanced at me then, eyes sharp. "You built a billion-dollar company, Lane. That means you've made enemies. I need to know who and why."

I exhaled slowly. I hated this. Hated how exposed I felt. But for once, I couldn't argue. These threats would be around until he figured it all out and put a stop to it. Then my life could go back to normal and that is what I wanted more than anything.

"Fine," I sighed. "Ask your questions."

The interrogation wasn't as painful as I expected. Blake didn't pry into emotions. He just wanted facts.

Who had access to my projects?

That was an easy one. It was under strict control with heavy levels of security. There were logs he could analyze to his heart's content.

Who would benefit from my downfall?

Try any competitor. They all wanted a piece of Lane Technologies. The undercurrent surrounding the buzz we had built around our latest software, Vanguard, had the industry on edge. It should. It was going to revolutionize cybersecurity. It had the potential to prevent unauthorized access into any system anywhere. We were launching within two weeks, and initial sales projections were through the roof.

Who did I trust?

The last question made me pause.

Blake caught it. "Not a long list, huh?"

I gave a short, humorless laugh. "Trust is dangerous."

Between competitors and the media always hounding after a story, preferably one with an element of scandal, I had learned to trust the person in the mirror and that was about the limit of it.

His gaze held mine for a beat longer than necessary. "So is being alone."

I looked away. "I've managed just fine."

Blake didn't argue. But something in his expression told me he wasn't convinced. Though I had a sneaking suspicion, his comment was from experience. His whole demeanor didn't invite people in. He was more the growling pit bull at the front door. I supposed that was a good persona for a bodyguard.

Hours passed, and to my surprise, the conversation turned less formal. I found myself talking. First, about the early days of my company: how I'd built it from nothing, how I'd spent years proving I deserved my success and had created the software we marketed. That it wasn't just some team of programmers somewhere. It was my designs, my influence, my direction. I made Lane Technologies.

Blake listened, really listened. He didn't interrupt, didn't offer hollow praise. Just absorbed every word. It was... unsettling. I was used to people spending more time thinking about what they were going to say next, usually how they wanted to impress me, than in what I was saying. Blake was paying attention. His deep brown eyes never left mine.

"You're not what I expected," he admitted.

I arched a brow. "And what did you expect?"

He smirked. "A spoiled, rich CEO who ignored threats."

I smirked back. "I am rich."

His gaze flickered to mine. "Yeah, but you're not spoiled."

The air between us shifted. It wasn't just guarded curiosity anymore. It was something else. Something neither of us was willing to name or even let our eyes meet for a few minutes. Somehow it had gotten personal. I wasn't sure what to make of it or if I should think about it at all. He was just my bodyguard, right? When this got resolved, he'd be gone. I needed to keep that in mind.

Later that night, as I sat in my home office reviewing security updates, a notification appeared on my screen. An encrypted message? That was odd. My blood ran cold. It was somehow addressed to me directly.

I know everything about you.

My heart started pounding. Who had been able to breach my security to send this to me? What did they know? Who was it? Who?

Blake was at my side in an instant. "What is it?"

My fingers trembled slightly as I turned the screen toward him. Blake's expression darkened as he read the words. This wasn't a random attack. It was straight at me, at home. This was personal. And whoever was behind it was already inside my world.

Blake's eyes scanned the message again, his jaw tightening. He straightened, stepping back from the screen, then pulled out his phone. "I need to run a trace on this."

I swallowed hard, my fingers tightening around the edge of my desk. "What if they already wiped their trail?"

"They probably did,' Blake admitted. "But that doesn't mean we don't look."

I exhaled sharply and stood, moving away from the desk and the message. The air in the penthouse felt heavy, suffocating. The message wasn't just a threat. It was a violation, a reminder that no matter how much control I thought I had, someone had just stripped it away. They had danced right into my home and shoved this under my nose.

I turned to Blake. "You were right."

His brows lifted slightly. "About?"

I hesitated. "About the threats not stopping."

Blake didn't gloat. He didn't smirk or say 'I told you so.' He just nodded. "Good. Now we deal with it."

I sighed and ran a hand over my hair. "How? I don't even know where to start."

"You let me do my job," he said. "And you stop pretending this is something you can handle alone."

That last part stung more than I expected. He had read me like a book when I thought I was concealed.

Blake worked for hours, coordinating with his contacts at Sierra Bravo, analyzing security footage, and reviewing system logs. I watched from a distance, unwilling to admit that his presence was oddly comforting. I never let anyone else take charge; yet here I was. Doing exactly that. Maybe it was because I wanted some distance between me and that message. I was not about to admit to throwing up my hands and tossing the problem at someone else to fix. Certainly not to a big, strong man. I fixed my own problems. Always had, always would. But this issue was something else. It made me feel under a microscope with nowhere to hide. I needed help coping with this invasion and Blake seemed to know exactly what to do. So, I let him while I regrouped.

At some point, I sat on the couch, curling up with my tablet to go over the launch plans for Vanguard, but I found myself distracted. By him. He spent part of the time pacing my apartment as he spoke on the phone, his movements precise, his focus absolute. The way he carried himself, the way he analyzed every angle. It was all muscle memory. Instinct. He was a warrior on a mission. It was impressive.

I had spent my career surrounded by intelligent, powerful people, but Blake was different. He didn't wield power the way businessmen did. He didn't use words to manipulate or charm. He just... was. A steady force. A presence that didn't demand attention but commanded it anyway. I hated that I noticed. And I hated even more that I liked it.

By the time Blake finally sat down, it was nearly two in the morning. He scrubbed a hand over his face. "The message was bounced through multiple encryption layers. No immediate trace."

I sighed as he confirmed what I had suspected. "So, we know nothing."

"Not nothing," Blake said. "They know a hell of a lot about computers and the phrasing—'I know everything about you', that's personal. They are saying this isn't just business."

A chill ran through me. "You think it's more than a competitor. That it may be someone close to me?"

Blake didn't answer right away. His gaze studied me carefully, like he was weighing how much truth I could handle. Finally, he said, "I think someone with inside access wants you to be afraid."

"Well," I said, rubbing my arms. "Mission accomplished." And I hated that worst of all.

For a long moment, neither of us spoke.

Then Blake exhaled. "You should get some sleep."

I let out a dry laugh. "Yeah, I'm sure that'll be easy after this."

He studied me again before standing. "Come on."

I blinked. "What?"

He nodded toward the hallway. "You're not sleeping out here. Go to your room. Lock the door. I'll be outside."

Something about the way he said it made my chest tighten. It wasn't an order. It wasn't condescending. It was... protective. And damn it, that made it worse. I was not a child to be herded off to bed. I nodded stiffly and turned, heading toward my room.

But even as I lay in bed, staring at the ceiling, I knew sleep wouldn't come. Because for the first time, I wasn't just afraid of the threats outside. I was afraid of how much I wanted to trust the man protecting me.

The next morning, I barely made it through my meetings without snapping at someone. My nerves were raw. The message had gotten under my skin in a way I hadn't expected, and Blake's constant presence only made it worse. Not because I didn't want him there. But because I did. It was a whole new experience for me, and I wasn't sure I liked it.

I was still lost in my thoughts when Blake fell into step beside me in the hallway. "You're quiet."

I shot him a look. "You complain when I talk, and now you complain when I don't?"

His mouth twitched. "Just making an observation."

I confessed. "I didn't sleep."

Blake nodded, unsurprised. "You need to start accepting that this isn't just a temporary problem. Whoever this is, they're not going away."

My stomach twisted. "I know."

For the first time, I fully accepted it. I wasn't safe. And I wasn't in control. The realization sat like lead in my chest.

Later that afternoon, an envelope appeared on my desk while I was away. I unfolded the enclosed note as I sat down.

You should have sold Vanguard when you had the chance. Now, it's too late.

"Danielle! Where did this come from?" I cried, hands shaking.

She rushed in from her desk and immediately shook her head, mystified. Blake took the note from me, his jaw tightening as he read it.

His eyes darkened with something dangerous as he recognized it had arrived despite every layer of security he had put in place.

"This wasn't just a breach," he snarled. "It's a warning."

I swallowed hard, feeling a chill. "What do you mean?"

"It means they can get to you anywhere," Blake said, scanning the office as if it had betrayed him. "And it means they're getting bolder."

I forced myself to stay steady, even as my pulse raced and I was tempted to run out of my own office. "What do we do now?"

Blake's gaze met mine.

"We find them," he said, voice low and lethal. "And we stop them before they get any closer."

This wasn't just about threats anymore. This was war. I was suddenly glad to have a soldier standing next to me. Blake's stance shifted, his eyes sweeping the office for any signs of how the note had gotten in. The thought of someone bypassing his security protocols must have burned at him. The threat wasn't just distant. It had gotten inside.

I exhaled shakily, pressing my fingers against my temples. "Whoever did this... they're not just trying to scare me, are they?"

Blake met my gaze. "No." His voice was firm. "They're testing boundaries. Seeing how far they can push before they make a move."

I took a breath before asking the next question. "And when they do?"

Blake's expression darkened. "Then I make mine."

The promise in his voice was enough to send a shiver down my spine. And for the first time, I wasn't sure who should be more afraid. My enemies. Or me.

Chapter 5
Breaking Down Walls
Blake Carter

I had protected a lot of people, but none had ever gotten under my skin quite like Avery Lane. It wasn't just the job. It was her.

The way she fought me at every turn. The way she refused to acknowledge the danger, even as the threats escalated. The way she carried the weight of an empire on her shoulders, pretending she didn't feel a thing.

I had spent years keeping my emotions out of my work. From the battlefield to Sierra Bravo, it kept me and my team alive and on mission. I had been fearless facing the enemy, assassins and all manner of threats. But with Avery, the professional and personal lines were starting to blur. And that was scary as hell.

Our morning started at Lane Technologies, where I ran another security check. I was relentless, checking the exits, scanning employee access logs, verifying encryption on Avery's communications. She tolerated it, but just barely. I think it was partially to compensate for these creeping feelings, but I worked all the harder. I was beyond pissed that someone had left a note on her desk. I was highly suspicious that it was someone who worked for her, maybe even her personal assistant. So far, I hadn't discovered the culprit.

"You're overthinking this," she said shaking her head as I checked the security cameras outside her office.

I didn't look up. "Someone left a threat on your desk yesterday. You still think I'm overthinking?"

She folded her arms, clearly annoyed. "Whoever they are, they want me rattled. I refuse to give them that."

Liar. She was covering.

I finally met her gaze. "And if they want more than that?"

A flicker of something crossed her face, fear, maybe. But just as quickly, she pushed it away. "Then we deal with it."

Oh. She said 'we'. Is this progress?

I exhaled. "You ever let anyone help you? Ever?"

"I don't need help," she said automatically.

I smirked. "Yeah, that's what I thought."

That afternoon, Avery took me to her research lab. The facility was sleek and modern, filled with top-tier engineers working on cutting-edge AI security solutions. The tech was impressive, but I was more interested in something else. The security was absolute garbage.

"You have millions of dollars in research here, and your access points are this weak?" I scowled as I analyzed the entry system. "Your encryption's solid, but your physical security is lacking."

Honestly, I would have preferred a concrete bunker with two armed guards at the only door compared to this glass and metal, easily accessible pretty building.

Avery frowned. "We have cameras. Badges. Motion detectors."

"Cameras and alarms don't stop people," I said. "Neither do badges if someone knows how to clone them."

Her lips pressed together. "No one's ever broken in before."

"They either haven't tried hard enough or haven't wanted to."

I walked the perimeter, noting weak spots. I could think of at least three ways to get past security without triggering alarms and I wasn't even thinking hard.

Avery followed me, watching me work. "You're really that paranoid?"

I turned to her. "I'm really that experienced."

She held my gaze. "What did you do before this?"

I hesitated. "Army. Special Forces."

Avery absorbed that, her expression unreadable. "Did you always want to be a soldier?"

I considered giving her some palatable lie but something about the way she asked made me answer honestly. "Didn't have much of a choice."

Something in her softened. "Me neither."

I frowned. "You didn't choose this?"

She let out a breath. "I built this company because I had to. Everywhere else, people loved my ideas so much, they stole them. I learned no one else was going to look out for me but me. It wasn't about money or success. It was about survival."

I studied her for a long moment. "That why you don't trust anyone?"

She gave a small smile. "You figure that out all on your own?"

My mouth twitched as she mimicked my sarcasm. "I'm observant."

The tension between us shifted. Not gone, but different. Less like a fight. More like an understanding.

By the time we left the lab, the sun had set. I drove us back to Avery's penthouse.

"Tell me what this Vanguard software can do." I said.

"It basically locks the barn door so no one can get in or out without authorization." She said.

"If I had it on my phone and I forgot my password, what then?"

She laughed. "Time for a new phone. In its current form it isn't meant for personal use though we have plans down the road. The launch version is for corporations to keep out ransomware, malware and the like."

"How good is it?"

"I invited a hacker group to have at it. They are still trying." She said with a touch of pride.

"What's the downside?" I said.

"Not sure." She said thinking, "I guess with some modifications, it would make the ultimate ransomware. No one could break it."

"How much is this bunch of code worth?" I asked as I pulled into her parking garage.

"Multiple billions by the CFOs estimate." She said with a canary eating grin.

"Now there's a reason to kill the creator." I said quietly.

My mind spun over to the weaknesses in her lab's security. That was the location where the Vanguard software was housed. If anyone was interested in it, that's where they'd hit.

"I'm going to tighten protocols at the lab," I said as we got out of the car.

Avery sighed. "You really can't turn it off, can you?"

"No," I said simply.

She shook her head but didn't argue. Inside, she poured herself a drink and settled onto the couch. I stayed standing, watching her.

"You ever take a break?" I asked.

She smirked. "You ever stop asking questions?"

I leaned against the windows. "Only when I get honest answers."

Avery studied me. "What do you want to know?"

I hesitated. Did she really mean that? Then, "Why do you live like this?"

She frowned. "Like what?"

"Like you're alone."

Avery tensed. "I'm not."

I didn't push. But I didn't believe her, either. Silence stretched between us.

Then, quietly, she said, "I don't have time for anything else."

I nodded slowly. "That's what I tell myself."

She looked at me, something unreadable in her gaze. "And?"

My voice was quiet. "And it's a lie. Everyone has 24 hours in a day and only so many of those to be alive in."

For the first time, she didn't have a response. We were still sitting there when my phone buzzed. I glanced at the screen and immediately straightened. "Motion alert at the lab."

Avery's breath hitched. "What?"

I was already moving. "Get to the car."

She didn't argue. When we arrived, the lab's security team was in disarray. Someone had tripped an internal alarm. That meant someone had bypassed the first layer of security and gotten inside undetected.

I pulled my gun as I entered, my focus razor-sharp. There had been no indication that the intruder had left the lab. A figure darted out of sight near the server room.

"Stay here," I ordered Avery.

I followed the shadow through the dimly lit corridor, every muscle coiled. Whoever they were, they were fast. But I was faster. They were undoubtedly headed for an exit. I went directly there. When the intruder hit the emergency exit, I was right behind them. I grabbed the figure just outside the door, slamming him against the wall. The hood fell. And my stomach dropped because I knew this guy. That meant things were worse than I thought. My grip tightened as I recognized Nathan Collins. A former soldier. A man I once trusted.

"You." I snarled.

Avery caught up just as I pressed Nathan harder against the wall. "Who is he?" she demanded.

My attention was split between wanting to interrogate Nathan and yell at Avery for coming after me when I had told her to stay back. I focused on Nathan. I'd deal with Avery later.

I didn't take my eyes off Nathan. "A mistake I thought I buried years ago."

Nathan let out a dry chuckle. "Miss me, Carter?"

I ignored the jab. "What the hell are you doing here?"

Nathan smirked. "Just admiring Lane's pitiful security."

Avery stiffened beside him. "You're behind this?"

Nathan tilted his head. "Let's just say I have an interest in how all this plays out."

My patience snapped. I twisted Nathan's arm, making him grunt in pain. Nathan was a mercenary. It's why we had crossed paths before. He was drug dealing back then. I had put him away years ago. I had thought he was still in prison. "Who hired you?" I growled.

Nathan gave a breathy laugh. "You're still the same, Carter. Always thinking brute force gets you answers."

I leaned in. "It will this time."

Nathan's smirk faltered. "You want to know who sent me? Ask your board. Though to get even with you, Blake, I did this one for free."

Avery inhaled sharply. "The board?"

My gut twisted. I didn't trust businessmen in general, but a betrayal at that level? I looked at Avery to gauge her reaction. He was saying I was partially to blame for her problems and so was her board. Nathan seized the moment of distraction, shoving off the wall. I had no time to adjust my hold before Nathan took off, sprinting toward the alley.

"Stay here," I ordered Avery again before taking off in pursuit.

Nathan was fast, but I was still faster. I tackled him near the fence, pinning him hard.

"Talk," I growled.

Nathan coughed, laughing through the pain. "You already know who to look at, Carter. That's why you're scared."

My hands twitched with the need to hit something. Sirens wailed in the distance. Security was closing in from the lab.

Nathan grinned. "We'll talk soon." Then, he slammed his head back into my jaw, breaking free just long enough to vanish into the night. I swore loudly. This was far from over.

Back at the penthouse, Avery paced. "My own board?" she frowned. "That doesn't make sense."

I sat on the edge of the couch, rubbing my bruised chin. I was more worried about how my history was playing some part in this and what I could do about it. "Makes perfect sense. If Vanguard launches, it changes everything. There's a lot of money in keeping the status quo."

Avery clenched her fists. "They wouldn't—"

I shot her a look. "You know them better than I do. Wouldn't they?"

Her silence was answer enough. Finally, she sank into the chair across from me.

"If they're involved, how do we prove it?"

I exhaled. "We start looking at their connections. Who benefits most if you are out of the picture?"

Avery's expression hardened. "Then we bring them down first."

I smirked. "Now you're thinking like a soldier."

Avery didn't smile. She just looked at me, something unreadable in her gaze.

"You trusted him once, didn't you?" she said.

I had been afraid she'd circle back to my connection to Nathan. She was too smart not to. My jaw clenched. "Doesn't matter now."

Avery studied me. "It does. Because now it's personal for both of us."

I didn't answer because she was right. And that was the problem.

I leaned forward, my elbows resting on my knees. "This isn't just business as usual anymore, Avery. If your own board is involved, they're not going to stop until they get what they want."

She exhaled, rubbing her temples. "And if what they want is me gone?"

My jaw tightened. "Then we make damn sure they don't get that chance."

Silence stretched between us, thick with something unspoken. Avery looked exhausted, but there was still fire in her eyes. Determination. Fear. And something else I couldn't quite put a name to.

"Why are you really doing this?" she asked softly.

I frowned. "What?"

"You could've just treated this like any other job. Left me here, taken me to the office in the morning. But you didn't."

I could have told her that wasn't the way I operated, and it would have been true to a point. I could have told her Sierra Bravo was the best in the business. We had never lost a client because we were vigilant and on the job 24/7. That would have been true too. But it wasn't what was driving me, and I knew it. My gut level reasons I was not willing to say aloud. Not even to myself.

Instead, I stood. "Get some rest, Lane. Tomorrow, we go hunting for big game."

And whoever was after her? They wouldn't see me coming.

Chapter 6
Uncovering Secrets
Avery Lane

Avery Lane

I had spent years building walls, metaphorical ones, reinforced with steel. But somehow, Blake Carter kept finding ways through them. I wasn't sure how it had happened. Maybe it was the way he took every threat seriously, refusing to brush off the danger. Maybe it was the way he challenged me, never letting me hide behind my usual defenses.

Or maybe it was because, for the first time, someone was standing beside me instead of watching from a distance waiting for me to fall so they could take advantage of me.

I hated how much I liked it because it was scary. He would go, leaving me without this feeling and I would miss it. Would I be missing him? I needed to focus. The launch was imminent. I had to barricade myself from these feelings, ignore him. Kind of impossible when he was always within sight!

Blake leaned against my desk, arms crossed. "If someone in your company is behind this, we need to find out who."

I let out a slow breath. "I still don't want to believe that."

"You don't have to believe it," Blake said. "You just have to be ready when we prove it."

I didn't argue. Not because I agreed, but because I was starting to realize he might be right.

The investigation started with my senior staff. Blake combed through access logs, financial records, and project files, searching for anything unusual. I sat beside him, sifting through years of company data.

Tensions in the company had been rising for months because of the imminent launch of Vanguard. There had been whispers of dissent, people who thought I was moving too fast, taking too many risks, pushing too hard to get things done. Employees who had been loyal once but now questioned my leadership. It was hard to stomach but I made myself go through the HR records. I wasn't looking for people to target. I was looking for someone targeting me.

He left on some errand, and I actually got to breathe on my own and not think about threats and betrayals for a few minutes. It was heady. Of course, that's when Warren Merrick strolled in. No email. No phone call. No notice at all. He just came in and settled into a chair in front of my desk like he owned the place. Sometimes, the man pissed me off. I plastered a big smile on my face.

"What brings the chairman in on this lovely day?" I asked.

It was pouring rain, dark and overcast. Perfectly matched my mood going through these files looking for betrayals. A drop-in visit by the board chair was just icing on the cake.

"Just wanted to check in on you, face to face, after that mess the other night." He said, looking concerned.

I shouldn't be surprised that he knew about the lab break-in. I saw Blake out of the corner of my eye, standing at my door, arms crossed, frowning as he looked at Merrick. Technically, Merrick had signed the contract with Sierra Bravo, Blake's employer. I had no idea what was making him frown.

"I'm fine. Blake had it all covered." I said, waving it away.

"I guess it was a good thing he was there." Warren said but there was no emotion behind his comment. I couldn't tell if he was happy about it or not. "With all this uproar, have you given any more thought to delaying the launch or better yet, I still have that investor who wants to buy Vanguard. We could avoid the potential downsides and take the big boost to our bottom line."

"We talked about this." I said, trying to maintain my patience. He was the chair. He was a major CEO in his own right. He wasn't a dweeb even though I felt like he was acting like one. "It would be a considerable one-time increase but that would be the end of it. We keep ownership, then we license it over and over for an ongoing income stream. I presented those numbers at the summer meeting."

"Uh-hmm. I remember. I'm just thinking about the headaches of upgrading it and the inevitable lawsuits when someone locks themselves out of their own systems."

"As you discussed at the time." I said. "The board voted against you." I said firmly.

I left it at that. I was not going to reargue this. Selling Vanguard for a penny when it was worth billions was stupid, and I was not stupid. If he kept pushing, I was going to suggest he leave the board if he was that worried. I didn't need this negativity when we were this close to launch.

"All right. I hear you, Avery. Just thought I'd see if I could change your mind. I'll let you get back to work." He said and gave me a smile. It didn't reach his eyes, and I wondered if he was trying to rally the board to his opinion. It was too late. We were too far along.

He left my office, walking by Blake. They didn't exchange greetings.

"I thought he'd be a cheerleader." Blake said, coming back to my desk to reopen his tablet.

"There's always at least one against anything you try to do." I sighed and went back to my screen.

"This isn't just about business anymore," Blake said still staring at his screen.

I frowned, trying to get my brain back on track. "What do you mean?"

He looked at me. "Someone doesn't just want your company. They want to ruin you."

A chill ran through me.

"What do you mean?" I asked, wondering what he was seeing.

"The tone of some of these. They want to take you down to their level, as if they don't believe you created the software but stole the ideas from someone else."

"That's not true!"

"Not saying it is." He said, pointing at the tablet in his hands, "But somehow it got into a few heads that it is. That's what vicious rumors do. They circle around the bottom where people don't know you and would rather believe in some good gossip than the truth. Happens all the time in politics."

"What do I do?"

"Talk to your PR department about an internal blitz to motivate your own people about Vanguard. That should quiet the rumor mill. I don't think it's where the threats come from but if you're seeing any glitches in your launch progress, it might be because of internal errors. Could be deliberate, might be accidental. A bit of internal advertising might help."

"I'll get Danielle on it." I said chewing my lip. The last thing I needed was Vanguard's launch grinding to a halt. Merrick would love that.

By midday, we had a list of potential suspects.

Blake glanced at me. "Who do you trust on this list?"

I hesitated. Before Nathan, I would have said everyone, at least to some degree. Today? I said, softly, "I don't know anymore."

His expression didn't change, but something flickered in his eyes. "Yeah," he said. "I know the feeling."

I studied him. "What happened to you?"

Blake exhaled, running a hand over his jaw. "Long story."

"I've got time," I said.

For a long moment, he didn't speak.

Then, finally, he said, "I trusted the wrong people. It cost me everything."

My chest tightened. "And you never trusted anyone again?"

Blake's gaze held mine. "Not until now."

The air between us stilled. It was like when I met with an investor, and you could tell when he was going to say yes. Blake and I had a moment of agreement. And it was both intimate and scary. I was the one to look away first.

That evening, we were still working in my office, trying to narrow the list. An employee, one of the names on our list actually, stormed into the office, demanding to talk.

Blake was at my side in an instant, body tense. "Stay behind me."

Cole, a mid-level manager, was red-faced with anger. "You think you can just push people out?" he spat.

I stood my ground. "I don't understand. If you have a problem, you can—"

Blake cut me off. "Step back, Lane."

I bristled, but for once, I listened.

Cole's fists clenched. "You don't know what you've started," he hissed.

Blake looked ready to fight. "What does that mean?"

Cole's eyes flickered, just for a second. That was all Blake needed. He moved fast, grabbing Cole's arm.

"Who are you working with?" Blake demanded.

Cole struggled, but Blake didn't let go. Cole was a tech manager. Blake was a soldier. It was no contest.

I stepped forward. "Tell me the truth, Cole. What's going on here? Who are you protecting?"

Cole's lips parted but then he caught himself. He ripped free and bolted. Blake swore and took off after him. Security and Blake caught Cole before he reached the elevator. Security dragged him back, but his expression had changed. Now, he looked afraid.

I stepped closer. "What do you know?"

Cole swallowed. "You don't get it. It's too late."

Blake snarled. "Too late for what?"

Cole hesitated. Then, finally, "They already have everything."

"Everything what?" I said, trying to keep from screaming it. This cryptic half telling me things was infuriating.

"I can't." Cole whimpered. "They took Jeffrey."

"Who?" I asked, bewildered.

"My son." Cole said, "If you don't give them what they want, I don't know what they'll do."

"Who are they? What do they want?" Blake demanded, "We'll get your son back."

Cole shook his head and refused to say anything more no matter what I promised or Blake threatened. After Cole was escorted out,

Blake locked down the office, running another deep dive into security footage. Blake was silent, angry. I sat beside him, mind racing.

My blood ran cold. Now whoever *they* were had added kidnapping, extortion and who knew what else. I had no idea what to do. Without knowing who was behind this or what they wanted other than me dead, it was impossible. This was definitely Blake's world – not mine. Then my phone buzzed. I pulled it out, heart pounding. Another encrypted message.

It's not just your company. It's you. We're closer than you think.

I looked at Blake. For the first time, I was truly afraid. I was paralyzed. Blake grabbed the phone from my hand, scanning the message. His jaw tensed, his grip tightening. "Damn it."

I inhaled sharply. "They must be inside, watching me."

Blake's voice was firm. "Then we find them before they make their next move."

I turned away, arms wrapping around myself. "I don't understand. If they have everything, why not use it? Why keep playing games?"

Blake's expression darkened. "Because they want you scared."

I swallowed hard. It was working.

"Someone on my board could be responsible," I admitted.

Blake glanced at me. "You really think one of them would betray you?"

I let out a humorless laugh. "Billion-dollar deals make people do ugly things. Like kidnapping a little boy."

Blake studied me. "And what about you?"

I frowned. "What about me?"

"How far would you go to protect what's yours?"

My eyes darkened. "As far as I have to."

Blake nodded. "Then you understand the people we're dealing with."

I hated that he was right. I wouldn't resort to kidnapping, extortion and murder but beyond that? The lines weren't very hard in the sand. Hours passed, but neither of us moved from the office. Blake combed through employee records, searching for any unusual patterns. I monitored network activity, trying to identify data breaches.

"You always work this late?" Blake asked after a while.

I smirked tiredly. "You always babysit your clients this closely?"

He shrugged. "Only when they attract this much trouble."

I sighed, rubbing my eyes. "I didn't ask for this."

Blake's voice was softer. "I know."

Something in his tone made my stomach flip. I pushed the thought away. I needed to concentrate on what I was doing. It was past midnight when I found something. It was in an internal log, an unauthorized transfer from my system, sent to an external device.

Blake leaned in. "That's not good."

My pulse quickened. "It's from an executive terminal."

Blake met my gaze. "Someone high up."

I swallowed. "Someone close to me."

We stared at the screen. Neither of us said it. But we were both thinking the same thing. The traitor wasn't just in my company. They were in my inner circle. And they were getting closer.

I leaned back in my chair, exhaling through my nose. The realization settled in my chest like a weight. Someone I had trusted, someone I had worked beside, had been feeding information to my enemies.

"Do you think it's one of the board members?" I asked, my voice quieter now.

Blake didn't answer right away. Instead, he studied the screen, scanning the timestamps and access logs. Finally, he said, "If I were betting, I'd say yes. But we need proof."

I let out a bitter laugh. "Proof. Right. Because it's not like someone just confessed in my office tonight."

Blake shook his head. "Cole was small-time. He said someone kidnapped his son, which means he was a pawn. Someone else is calling the shots."

I rubbed my temples. "So, what do we do?"

Blake looked at me, something sharp and determined in his gaze. "We set a trap."

The next morning, I walked into my office with Blake trailing behind me, looking every bit like a shadow I couldn't shake.

"You don't have to hover," I said quietly.

"Yeah, I do," he replied easily.

Danielle, my assistant, looked up from my desk, her face tight with concern. "Ms. Lane, I took a look at the new security measures Mr. Carter requested. They're... extensive."

I sighed. "I'm aware "

Blake smirked. "Just wait until you see phase two."

Danielle blinked, then turned back to me. "There's something else. Your CFO, Roger Whitman, called. He wants an emergency meeting. Says it's important."

My stomach twisted. Roger had been with the company since the beginning. I had been to his wedding, his daughter's christening, their annual Christmas parties. But if anyone had insider access, it had to be the Chief Financial Officer. He was also on the board.

Blake caught the shift in my expression. "Something wrong?"

I forced a neutral tone. "No. Let's see what Roger has to say."

An hour later, we sat across from Roger in one of the conference rooms. He looked nervous, his fingers drumming against the table, his eyes darting between me and Blake.

"I don't know how to say this," Roger started. "But I think someone inside the company is leaking data."

Blake and I exchanged a glance.

"Go on," I said carefully.

Roger exhaled. "There have been inconsistencies in our financial reports. Transfers that don't add up. And last night, I found this."

He slid a flash drive across the table.

Blake picked it up, narrowing his eyes. "What is it?"

"Logs," Roger said. "Proof that someone on the board has been making unauthorized charges. I don't know who yet, but—"

The lights flickered. Then the conference room door locked with an audible *click*. Blake was on his feet instantly, reaching for his weapon. I stood too, heart pounding.

"What the hell—" Roger started.

Then my phone buzzed. I looked down. A single message flashed across the screen.

You're too late.

Seeing it, Blake cursed under his breath. "We need to move. Now."

I barely had time to process before he was grabbing my wrist, pulling me toward the emergency exit. Because whoever was behind this? They weren't just watching anymore. They were making their next move.

Chapter 7
Dangerous Liaisons
Blake Carter

I knew better than to ignore my gut. Right now, my gut was telling me that I was running out of time. Whoever was behind the attacks on Avery wasn't just playing games anymore. They were making moves, escalating. The message in the conference room had been a warning. The next one wouldn't be.

Which was why I was here, sitting in a darkened corner of a bar that smelled like whiskey and regret, waiting for a man who might have answers.

Hale arrived fifteen minutes late, as usual. I barely looked up as my old Army contact slid into the seat across from me wearing his antique jean jacket with its varied patches from rock bands. His hair was a shaggy rusty brown mess barely competing with his full beard and mustache.

"You look like hell," Hale chuckled.

I smirked. "Still prettier than you."

Hale snorted. "What do you need, Sargeant?"

I didn't waste time. "I need intel. Fast."

Hale's expression darkened. "This about the Lane situation?"

I stilled. "You already know?"

Hale nodded. "You think you're the only one watching her?"

My stomach twisted. "Who else is looking?"

Hale leaned in. "That's the problem, man. It's not just one group. It's multiple players."

Hale was a hacker of some repute who followed tech gossip and news like some people tracked the royals of England. He knew everything about everybody or claimed to. It's why I was here. That and serving together in some god-awful sandy place long ago.

I exhaled. "Give me names."

Hale shook his head. "I don't have that. Not yet. But I can tell you this. Whoever is after her? It's multiple fronts, man: competition, internal and personal."

I clenched my jaw. I had suspected at least competitive and internal. The last was a new one. Not that we needed any more to deal with.

"How personal?"

Hale hesitated. "I don't know yet. But if I were you? I'd start looking at people who have a reason to hate you, not just her."

I frowned. "Me? You mean Nathan Collins?"

Hale met my gaze. "And bingo was his name-o. But there are more skeletons coming out of the woodwork. I am having so much fun with this."

"Yeah. A real blast for Avery, too. If you find out more, I need it ASAP. Got it?"

"You are on my speed dial, Sarg." Hale said lifting the beer I had gotten for him.

By the time I left the bar, my mind was racing. If there were more people from my past coming, then the game had changed. I moved through the side streets, my instincts on high alert. Then I heard it. A footstep. Too close. Too deliberate. I didn't hesitate. I turned, reaching for my weapon—

Too late.

Something slammed into me from behind, knocking the breath from my lungs. I staggered, as I twisted, throwing a punch blindly into the darkness. My fist connected with flesh.

A grunt. A curse.

Then another body collided with mine.

I fought, my muscles burning as I grappled against unseen attackers. I managed to throw one off, but another came at me from the side, a sharp pain slicing across my ribs.

A knife.

Damn it.

I dropped low, using the momentum to take my attacker down. The other one was already running.

I let them go. I had bigger problems. My side was bleeding. And I still didn't have answers. I pressed a hand to my ribs, feeling the warmth of blood seep through my shirt. It wasn't deep, more of a warning cut than a kill shot. Amateurs. But amateurs who didn't operate alone. Who the hell was pulling the strings?

I forced myself to move, ignoring the sting as I made my way to my car. My vision swam slightly, but I gritted my teeth and powered through it. I needed to get back to Avery. By the time I reached her penthouse, the adrenaline was fading, leaving behind exhaustion and pain. I didn't bother using the elevator. I took the stairs two at a time, forcing my body to keep up. When I reached the door, I knocked once. Avery answered immediately, eyes widening when she saw me.

"What the hell happened to you?"

I pushed past her. "Long night."

She grabbed my arm, stopping me. "You're bleeding."

I sighed. "Noticed that, did you?"

Avery ignored my sarcasm. "Sit. Now."

I wasn't about to argue. Minutes later, I was sitting on her couch, shirtless, as she pressed a damp cloth against my wound. Her touch was surprisingly gentle, but her expression was anything but.

"Who did this?" she asked.

I studied her face. "I don't know yet."

She exhaled sharply. "You're supposed to be the one keeping *me* safe, not the other way around."

I smirked. "You worried about me, Lane?"

She scowled. "Don't flatter yourself."

But she didn't pull away.

I let the silence stretch between us. I could feel her pulse thrumming through her fingertips where she held the cloth to my ribs. She was close. Too close. I needed to do something distracting.

I cleared my throat. "I met with an old contact. I confirmed what we already suspected. This isn't just about your company. It's personal."

Avery stilled. "Personal how?"

I hesitated. "He thinks I might be part of the reason you're in danger."

Her brow furrowed. "You? You mean that Nathan person."

I nodded. "I've made enemies, Lane. Him. Maybe others. Some of them don't let go."

Avery studied me for a long moment. Then, softly, she said, "Tell me."

I clenched my jaw. "You don't want to know."

She reached for my hand, surprising us both. "Try me."

For the first time in a long time, I wanted to. I told her about my past. About the mission that had gone sideways. About the choices

I had made that had cost men their freedom or their lives. Avery listened, silent.

When I finished, she simply said, "It wasn't your fault."

I let out a bitter chuckle. "You sound sure about that."

She met my gaze. "Because I know what guilt looks like. And I know what regret sounds like. You're carrying both."

My throat tightened. I wanted to look away. But I couldn't. The moment broke when Avery's phone buzzed. She pulled it out, and I immediately saw the shift in her expression.

"What is it?" I asked.

She turned the screen toward me. Another message.

You're not the only one with secrets.

My blood ran cold.

"Someone's watching us," she whispered.

My jaw clenched. "Not for long."

We spent the next hour tracing the message. I worked fast, cross-referencing IP addresses, analyzing patterns.

"This isn't a random hacker," I announced. "They know exactly what they're doing."

Avery sat beside me, her arms crossed tightly. "What do they want?"

My stomach twisted. "They want control. And they're getting closer."

She exhaled. "So, what do we do?"

I looked at her. And in that moment, I made a decision.

"We stop waiting," I said. "We take the fight to them."

Avery nodded. She was done being afraid. And so was I. My mind worked in overdrive. Whoever was behind this wasn't just playing games anymore. They were getting bolder, and now they had shifted their focus. I wasn't just protecting Avery anymore. I was a target, too.

"We need to change the plan," I said, shutting my laptop with a sharp click.

Avery frowned. "What do you mean?"

"I mean, we stop reacting and start setting traps." I leaned forward. "Whoever this is, they're watching our every move. But we can use that against them."

Avery hesitated. "You're talking about baiting them out."

"Exactly," I said. "We need to force their hand. Give them an opportunity to make a mistake."

She exhaled. "And what if it backfires?"

My gaze darkened. "Then I make sure they don't get a second chance."

Avery studied me. Her expression was unreadable. Then she said, "What do you need from me?"

I smirked. "You really trust me now, huh?"

She rolled her eyes. "Don't push it."

But she didn't say no. And that was enough. The plan came together quickly. We would announce a sudden press conference, an exclusive update on Vanguard. Something high-profile, something impossible for the enemy to ignore.

"We make it look like you're moving forward as if nothing's wrong," I explained. "They won't be able to resist making a move."

Avery nodded slowly. "And you'll be waiting for them."

My expression hardened. "Damn right I will."

She tapped her fingers against the desk, lost in thought. Then, softly, she said, "Be careful, Blake."

It wasn't an order. It wasn't a demand. It was something else entirely. I felt it settle in my chest.

"I will," I promised.

And for the first time, I wasn't just saying it for her sake.

That night, as I stood watch outside Avery's room, I felt something shift inside me. This wasn't just a job anymore. This was war. And I wasn't going to lose. The stakes were too high. There was a beautiful woman just on the other side of that door who was depending on me to not only keep her safe but also her company and to a certain extent, whatever this little fragile thing was between us that had her telling me to be careful as if I were important to her as a person, as more than a bodyguard.

I stood by the window, staring out at the city below. The skyline stretched far and wide, but somewhere in that vast expanse, our enemy was watching. Waiting. Just like I was.

My fingers tapped lightly against my side. The wound still stung, but it was nothing compared to the unease crawling under my skin. I had been hunted before, on battlefields, in the shadows of places I never wanted to return to.

But this was different. This wasn't just my life on the line. It was Avery's.

A soft sound behind me made me turn. Avery stood in the doorway, wrapped in a silk robe, her expression unreadable.

"You should rest," she said quietly.

I exhaled. "So, should you."

Neither of us moved. Neither of us slept. Because the war had only just begun.

Chapter 8
The Reckoning
Avery Lane

I had never been afraid of danger. But watching Blake Carter bleed? That was different.

He sat on my couch, his shirt discarded, the harsh light casting shadows over his muscled torso. The wound on his ribs wasn't deep, but it was enough to make my stomach tighten. He had been attacked because of me. Because he was doing his job protecting me.

And that realization unsettled me more than anything.

"You should see a doctor," I said, voice tight.

Blake smirked. "You volunteering?"

Breaking my own rule, I rolled my eyes but didn't step back. I pressed a clean cloth against the wound, feeling the tension in his muscles as I did.

"You're reckless," I whispered.

Blake exhaled. "Comes with the job."

I swallowed, forcing myself to focus. "This isn't just a job, is it?"

His gaze locked onto mine. "Not anymore."

And just like that, the air between us changed.

The next morning, I sat at the office conference table, staring at the names in front of me. Board members. Executives. People I had trusted.

Blake stood beside me, arms crossed. "Someone on this list is playing you."

I shook my head. "I don't want to believe that."

"I know," Blake said. "But we don't have the luxury of denial."

I studied the names. "Roger said he found financial discrepancies. What if it's not just money they're after?"

Blake's jaw tightened. "Then they want *you* out of the picture."

The weight of it settled over me. Someone close to me wanted me gone. And I had no idea who. The investigation took hours. We analyzed bank records, security footage, confidential reports. Slowly, patterns began to emerge

Blake tapped the screen. "Here. Transactions that don't make sense. Offshore accounts."

I frowned. "And look at the timing. Right before each big attack, someone withdrew large sums."

Blake's voice was grim. "They're funding this with your own money."

My stomach turned. "Which means they're not working alone. They're paying people on the outside."

Blake met my gaze. "We're dealing with a network."

I exhaled. "And someone on my team is at the center of it."

I had never felt so exposed.

Later that evening, I found myself standing by the penthouse window, looking out over the city.

Blake watched me from the doorway. "You okay?"

I turned. "No."

He didn't say anything He just waited.

I bit my lip. "I can handle threats. I can handle competitors trying to tear me down. But this? Someone I trust betraying me?" I let out a shaky breath. "I don't know how to deal with that."

Blake stepped closer. "You don't have to do it alone."

I looked up at him. "That's the problem."

His brows furrowed. "What?"

I hesitated. "Your being here. My trusting you. It terrifies me more than any of this."

Blake's expression softened. "Why?"

I swallowed and let the truth out. "Because I don't let people in. And somehow, you got past every wall I've built."

Blake was quiet for a moment. Then he said, "Maybe they weren't as strong as you thought."

My breath hitched. I had no response. Before either of us could speak, my phone buzzed. Another damned message. Blake leaned in as I read it.

It's time. You won't see it coming.

A chill ran down my spine. I wanted to throw the phone off the balcony.

Blake grabbed his gun. "We need to move. Now."

My heart pounded. The reckoning had begun. My fingers tightened around the phone as I read the message again. *It's time. You won't see it coming.* I had spent years preparing for threats: business rivalries, corporate espionage, even the occasional legal battle. But this? This was different.

Blake moved fast, his body shifting into motion as he secured the doors and checked his gun. "We're leaving."

I exhaled sharply. "Where?"

"Somewhere safe." His voice was clipped, authoritative. "Whoever sent this isn't bluffing. We need to be ahead of them."

I hesitated. "And running fixes what, exactly?"

Blake turned, his dark gaze locking onto mine. "It keeps you alive."

I wanted to argue. To tell him I wasn't the kind of woman who ran. But the truth was, for the first time in my life, I had no idea what the next move should be and at least Blake had a plan. So, I did something I never thought I'd do. I let Blake take the lead.

Twenty minutes later, we were in an armored SUV, speeding through the city. Blake drove, his hands firm on the wheel, eyes flicking to the rearview mirror every few seconds. His phone was on speaker, connected to a contact I didn't know.

"Tell me you've got something," Blake said.

A happy sounding voice responded. "Whoever sent that message rerouted it through six different servers. Someone with resources."

I folded my arms. "So, it's not just some rogue hacker."

"No," Blake said. "This is calculated."

I exhaled. "And you still think it's someone in my company?"

Blake hesitated. "I think it's someone who knows you personally. Someone who wants to see you fall."

I shook my head. "Then why keep warning me?"

Blake's grip on the wheel tightened. "Because they don't just want to take your company, Lane. They want to break you first."

A chill ran through me as Blake pulled into a private garage beneath an unmarked building.

I glanced around as he parked. "Where are we?"

"Safe house," he said. "No one knows about it."

I followed him inside, taking in the stark surroundings, minimal furniture, weapons tucked into compartments, reinforced doors, computer screens cycling through exterior views.

"This is yours?" I asked.

Blake nodded. "Not personally. Sierra Bravo's. One of them."

I swallowed. "They maintain these kinds of places?"

He smirked. "We plan ahead."

I studied him for a moment. "What brought you to this, Blake?"

He sighed, running a hand through his hair. "A lot."

I didn't press. Not yet.

Instead, I turned to the window, staring at the city skyline. "You think they'll come after me tonight?"

Blake's voice was steady. "I know they will."

I should have been terrified. But somehow, with him standing there and after everything that had happened, I wasn't. Hours passed. I sat on the couch, my arms wrapped around myself. Blake stood near the window, silent and alert.

Finally, I spoke. "This is insane."

Blake glanced at me. "Which part?"

I let out a dry laugh. "All of it. My life. The fact that I have a bodyguard. That I'm hiding in a safe house." I exhaled. "That you're the only person I trust right now."

Blake's gaze softened. "I get it."

I looked at him. "Do you?"

He nodded. "More than you know."

For a moment, the tension between us wasn't about danger. It wasn't about survival. It was something else. Something neither of us was ready to name. Then my phone buzzed. I did not want to look at it. A new message. Blake was at my side in an instant. I unlocked the screen, heart pounding, groaning. The message was simple.

You should have run when you had the chance.

Blake swore under his breath. "They must know where we are."

My breath caught. Blake moved instantly, securing the room, checking the surveillance feeds from his phone. His movements were quick, efficient. Controlled. I, on the other hand, felt my pulse hammering in my throat.

"How?" I whispered.

Blake's expression was grim. "Someone leaked our location."

I stiffened. "You think it was someone from your team?"

Blake hesitated, then shook his head. "No. But I think they have someone watching you. Someone close enough to know your every move."

I swallowed hard. "This isn't just about me anymore, is it?"

Blake met my gaze. "No. They want me out of the way, too."

I hugged myself, trying to process the reality of our situation. "We can't just sit here."

Blake nodded. "We won't." He handed me a small earpiece. "From now on, you don't go anywhere without this. If I say run, you run. With this, I will find you."

I took it, my fingers brushing his. "Blake..."

His gaze softened just slightly. "I swear we'll get through this, Lane."

I nodded, gripping the earpiece but deep down, I wasn't sure either of us truly believed it. Minutes later, the security cameras flickered. Blake's muscles tensed.

I stared at my phone screen with its latest damning message. "They're here."

Blake grabbed his weapon. "Stay behind me."

Footsteps echoed in the hall. I clenched my fists. I had spent my life fighting for control. But tonight? Tonight, control was gone from my grasp. And whoever was on the other side of that door? They were here to take everything.

My breath came in short, shallow bursts. The room felt smaller, the walls pressing in as the footsteps outside grew closer. Blake's body was a shield in front of me, his stance rigid, weapon raised and aimed at the door.

Then. Silence.

The kind that made my skin prickle. Blake motioned for me to stay low. He moved toward the door, every motion precise, controlled. He cracked it open a fraction, enough to see into the hallway.

A shadow moved.

Blake tensed. "They're trying to flank us."

My pulse thundered. "What do we do?"

Blake's voice was steady. "We fight."

The door handle turned. I held my breath.

And then, the attack began.

Chapter 9
Trust Issues
Blake Carter

I didn't trust easily. And right now, I trusted no one.

The safe house had been compromised. We had to take the underground exit. The enemy wasn't just watching. They were here. The security feed showed shadows outside. Avery stood beside me, tense but composed. She was good at hiding fear, but I had learned to read her. We took the underground exit to a different SUV and made our escape.

"They want us rattled," she said.

I nodded. "And they're doing a damn good job of it."

At least I knew this vehicle was not geotagged. We went on to safe house beta. There was only one move left. We had to take the fight to them. An hour later, we had a plan. Avery's security logs showed unauthorized access to internal systems. Whoever was behind it had been feeding our every move to the enemy.

And he had a name.

Derek Marshall. Executive Advertising VP. Trusted advisor. Now, a suspect. I wasn't surprised. Avery, though, looked like she wanted to be sick.

"He was at my side for years," she murmured.

My jaw tightened. "That's how they get close."

Avery swallowed. "What do we do?"

My voice was firm. "We confront him."

She exhaled. "And if he's working with them?"

My grip tightened on my gun. "Then we end this."

We found Derek at his home, a sleek high-rise of largely glass in the city. He had some kind of security system. I circumvented it the simplest way. I kicked in the door. Derek barely had time to react before I had him pinned against the wall. He was largely a mid-fifties pencil pusher. Not exactly in my league.

"What the hell?" Derek sputtered.

My voice was low. Dangerous. "You've got one shot, Marshall. Tell me why you sold Avery out."

Derek's eyes darted to Avery. "You think I—"

I pressed harder. "We have proof."

Derek's face paled.

Avery stepped closer. "Why, Derek?"

His lips parted. Then, suddenly, he shoved me back, breaking free. I reacted instantly, grabbing him again, slamming him onto the table.

"Talk," I growled.

Derek coughed. "I ... I was paid."

Avery's voice was ice. "By who?"

Derek hesitated.

I twisted his arm. "Don't make me ask again."

Derek groaned. "The board. They—"

A gunshot rang out. A window shattered. I hit the ground, covering Avery. A sniper. I glanced back at Derek and saw brains. Derek was dead or as good as.

I cursed. "Move!"

We ran. Bullets tore through the walls as they came through the glass windows. The enemy wasn't hiding anymore. They were covering their tracks. I dragged Avery toward the hallway, keeping my body between her and the clear windows. My instincts screamed at me to move faster, but every step felt like a calculated risk. The sniper had a clean shot. If we hesitated, we were dead. We reached the stairwell, slamming the door behind us.

Avery's breath was sharp. "Derek was our only lead."

I gritted my teeth. "He was a loose end. They tied it up."

She swallowed hard. "How did they know we'd be here?"

"They're watching everything." I said.

"How many people do they have?" she whispered, eyes large.

I scanned our surroundings. "Enough and now they know we're hunting them."

Since they seemed to be one step ahead, I headed back to the penthouse. I secured the doors and lowered the blinds. I checked my weapon, then turned to Avery.

"You okay?" I asked.

She nodded, but I didn't buy it. She might as well have said 'fine'.

I exhaled. "This doesn't end until we take them down."

Avery's voice was quiet. "And what happens after?"

I stilled. After? That was a loaded word. I hadn't thought that far ahead. For the first time, I realized the thought of not seeing Avery after the job was over left me feeling empty. And that scared me a hell of lot more than a sniper.

The next day, Avery was unusually quiet. I watched her, noting the tension in her jaw. I could tell she was trying to push through the emotions, trying to keep herself together.

Finally, she sighed. "I."

I raised a brow. "Yeah?"

She hesitated. "Last night... I realized something."

I leaned forward. "What?"

She met my gaze. "I'm not afraid of dying. I'm afraid of needing someone."

My chest tightened. I knew that feeling. Intimately. I was afraid of this topic of conversation, too.

I swallowed hard. "You already do."

Avery's breath hitched. Neither of us moved. Then, slowly, I reached out, brushing a stray strand of hair from her face. She didn't pull away. The kiss was inevitable.

The tension had been there for days, simmering beneath every argument, every touch. I knew it was dangerous. But when Avery leaned in, I didn't stop her. Her lips were soft, hesitant at first, then more certain. My hands found her waist, pulling her closer, feeling the heat of her body against mine. For a moment, nothing else mattered. Not the threats. Not the danger. Just her. And the electric magic of those incredible soft lips.

Then the phone rang.

I pulled back, my breathing uneven. I reached for my phone, answering without taking my eyes off Avery.

A distorted voice spoke. "They're coming for the tech conference. You have forty-eight hours."

My grip tightened. "Who is this?"

The line went dead. I turned back to Avery. Our moment was gone. I read it in her eyes as surely as she saw it in mine. Reality had returned. And the countdown had begun. I lowered the phone. The tech conference was one of the biggest events in the industry, a public stage where Avery would be exposed. And now, it was a target.

Avery watched me carefully. "What did they say?"

I clenched my jaw. "The attack is coming in forty-eight hours."

She exhaled. "The conference. Then we need to cancel."

I shook my head. "No. If we back down, they win."

Avery crossed her arms. "If I go, I'm walking into a trap."

I took a step closer. "Then we set one of our own."

Her gaze searched mine. "And if they come for me?"

My voice was low. "They won't get the chance."

We spent the next day preparing. I coordinated with my team, making sure Avery's movements would be secure, controlling every detail of the event. I had one goal: eliminate the threat before they made their move.

Avery, meanwhile, played her part. She stepped in front of the cameras, faced the media, acted as if she weren't being hunted. I watched her from the sidelines, my pulse steady. She was brave. Too damn brave. And if anything happened to her, I didn't know what I'd do. It went way past the career ruining potential of a bodyguard losing a client. It had become personal.

The night before the conference, Avery found me on her penthouse balcony. The city stretched beneath us, lights flickering like stars.

She leaned against the railing. "You never stop, do you?"

I glanced at her. "What do you mean?"

She gave me a small smile. "Planning. Calculating. Protecting."

I looked away. "That's my job."

Avery studied me. "Is that all it is?"

I exhaled, rubbing the back of my neck. "I don't know anymore."

She turned to face me. "I."

I looked at her then, really looked.

Avery stepped closer. "I don't need a bodyguard."

I smirked. "Could've fooled me."

She shook her head. "I need *you*."

My breath caught. For a moment, I forgot about the job. Forgot about the threats. There was only her. And then—

A gunshot shattered the night.

I reacted instantly, pulling Avery down, shielding her with my body. Another shot rang out, sparking against the balcony railing.

I cursed. "We're compromised!"

Avery's breath was ragged. "You think?" she said, imitating my sarcasm.

I pulled my gun, my eyes scanning the rooftops, though I was outgunned against a sniper with a rifle. "We need to move. Now."

Avery nodded, gripping my hand. The war had come to our doorstep. I guided Avery inside, keeping her close as I secured the exits. My mind worked fast, calculating our next move. Whoever had fired those shots wasn't just sending a warning, they were trying to finish this.

Avery clutched my arm. "What now?"

My voice was steady. "We go dark."

She frowned. "Meaning?"

"We disappear. No phones. No contacts. We use their attack to make them think we're out of options."

Avery's pulse raced. "And then?"

My eyes darkened. "Then we make them regret ever coming after you."

We moved fast, slipping out through a service entrance, blending into the night. I led us to one of several unregistered vehicles I had

Sierra Bravo send over, keeping our movements unpredictable. Then we went to yet a different safe house: Charlie.

Avery sat beside me, her face pale but determined. "Do you ever get tired of this?"

I didn't look away from the road. "Of what?"

"Running. Fighting. Never knowing who to trust."

I exhaled. "You get used to it."

She studied me. "I don't want to."

I glanced at her then, my grip tightening on the wheel. "I won't let them take that choice from you."

Avery swallowed. "And what about you?"

I hesitated. "What about me?"

She reached over, resting a hand on my arm. "Who do *you* trust, Blake?"

My throat tightened. The answer should've been no one. But when I looked at her, I realized, it was her. Always her. And it made my heart skip a beat when I recognized the weight of that, the tug to get closer than a bodyguard ever should but it was far too late to back away now.

My new phone buzzed. A blocked number.

I answered, my voice sharp. "Talk."

A distorted voice spoke. "It's not over. The conference is the beginning. Be ready."

The line went dead. I met Avery's gaze. My grip tightened around the phone. The words echoed in my head. The conference is the beginning. Of what?

Avery watched me, her brows furrowed. "Who was it?"

I exhaled. "Someone who knows more than they should."

Her lips pressed together. "So, what do we do?"

I met her gaze. "We walk into that conference."

Avery inhaled sharply. "And if it's a trap?"

My voice was firm. "Then we spring it first."

Chapter 10
Emotions Unraveled

Avery Lane

I had spent years mastering control. Control over my company, over my emotions, over the expectations placed upon me. But one stolen moment, one kiss, had shattered the illusion. Blake Carter had kissed me. And worse? I had kissed him back. Now, in the cold light of morning, I couldn't ignore the consequences. Not just the danger we faced, but the weight of what I was feeling. I wasn't supposed to feel anything. And yet, I did. Blake stood across the room, leaning against the counter with a fresh cup of coffee. He looked unaffected, but I knew better.

I took a steadying breath. "About last night—"

Blake cut me off. "It was a mistake."

I flinched. That wasn't what I wanted to hear but I wasn't sure what it was that I expected. I was just his job, wasn't I? But that kiss ...

He ran a hand over his jaw, exhaling. "That's not what I meant."

I folded my arms. "Then what did you mean?"

Blake hesitated. "I mean, we can't afford distractions."

I forced myself to nod like it was of no consequence. I knew how to lie, too. "Right."

But deep down, I knew it wasn't that simple. Not anymore. Rather than enter that minefield, we focused on the conference. Since dealing with death threats was a much safer topic.

Blake had spent the night finalizing a security plan. I would attend as planned, under the guise of normalcy. But this time, Blake wouldn't just be my bodyguard. He would be my date, my armed candy, my shadow.

"We'll move in tandem," Blake said, mapping out our movements. "I won't be more than five feet from you at any time."

I arched a brow. "Sounds suffocating."

Blake smirked. "You'll live."

I exhaled. "I was kidding. And if they make their move?"

Blake's eyes darkened. "We make ours first."

I nodded. The plan was set. Now, all we had to do was survive.

The morning of the conference arrived faster than I would have liked. I stood in front of my mirror, smoothing the fabric of my tailored black dress. It was sleek, professional, armor for the battlefield I was about to walk into. I was used to it on some level. The posturing, the CEO in her element but not with the dark undercurrent that had presented itself.

My stomach twisted. Not because of the conference. Not because of the looming threat. But because of the man standing at my side. Blake was silent as he adjusted his cufflinks, the tension between us thicker than ever. The change from his usual old brown leather jacket, black t-shirt and jeans to this striking black tailored suit had nearly made my mouth drop open. Blake was suddenly incredibly handsome and appealing, and I was forcing back all kinds of inappropriate thoughts. He filled out that suit the way most men wished they could, and the tantalizing whiff of his cologne was almost making me wish for an old-fashioned Southern belle fan.

We hadn't spoken about the kiss since that morning. Every glance, every touch, carried an unspoken weight, an electricity now. I hated it. I hated the uncertainty, the vulnerability. And now, with his added curb appeal, I just wanted to slap him or rip him out of that suit. I wasn't sure which. Maybe both.

I turned to face him. "Are you ready?" I asked coolly.

Blake met my gaze. "Always."

And just like that, the conversation was over. The ride was tense.

The tech conference was a spectacle of flashing lights and eager investors. I had been through a hundred of these before, shaking hands, making deals, proving why I was the best. And everyone wanted to hear about Vanguard. It was the latest buzz thanks to our carefully outlined promotion plan, scheduled to coincide with this year's tech conference.

But, even so, today was different. Today, I wasn't just here to impress. I was here to be a target but to survive. Blake stayed close, his presence a constant pulse of awareness against my skin. I could feel his eyes scanning every corner, his body attuned to any sign of danger. I should have felt safer. Instead, I felt exposed.

"Breathe," Blake whispered beside me, his warm fingers against my forearm.

I shot him a look. "I am breathing."

Blake smirked. "Could've fooled me."

I exhaled sharply. "I hate you."

His smirk deepened. "No, you don't."

And that was the problem. His fingertips were sending chills down my arm. The tension only grew as the day progressed. I was used to being in control, but Blake's proximity threw me off balance. Every time he placed a hand on my back to guide me through a crowd, every time our arms brushed, a spark ignited beneath my skin. I told myself it was adrenaline. It wasn't. By the time we reached the main stage, I was drowning in it.

Blake leaned in, his breath warm against my ear. "It's almost showtime."

I swallowed. "Let's get this over with."

I lifted my skirt to go up the steps leading to the stage, my heart hammering.

And then—

All hell broke loose.

The explosion wasn't loud, but it was enough. Enough to send a crowd accustomed to the nightly terror news into chaos. Enough to tell us the attack had begun.

Blake was already moving.

"Go," he barked, grabbing my arm and pulling me into motion.

Security swarmed, pushing people toward the exits. They were Blake's team; so, they were good, controlled, responsive. My mind raced, trying to process the situation. Figure out a safe path. See who might be an enemy. Why did I bother? Blake was way ahead of me. Then I saw him. A man in the crowd, too still, too calm. My stomach dropped.

"Blake?" I gasped.

Blake followed my gaze. The man reached into his jacket. Blake shoved me behind him as a gunshot rang out. Screams filled the air. And the real fight began.

Blake reacted. He grabbed me, twisting us both to the ground as a second bullet sailed past, shattering the plastic podium behind us. The crowd screamed again, surging toward the exits in a frenzied stampede. Chaos reigned despite security's efforts.

Blake rolled, pulling me up with him. "We're moving!"

I barely registered what was happening. My pulse was deafening in my ears, my hands trembling. I had been in high-stakes meetings, had stared down ruthless executives, but nothing, *nothing*, had ever felt like this, being shot at. Like close up life or death.

Blake shoved me behind a row of chairs. "Stay low," he ordered. I swallowed hard, nodding as another shot rang out. Blake cursed under his breath. He could see the shooter now, moving with practiced ease, cutting through the chaos like a predator stalking its prey. And his target was me.

Blake gritted his teeth. "Not happening."

He left me, moving fast, dodging through the crowd, using the fleeing bodies as cover. He closed the distance just as the gunman raised his weapon again. Blake lunged. My heart was in my throat. But it wasn't fear for me. I was afraid for Blake.

The impact sent Blake and the man crashing into a display stand. The gun skidded across the floor. The attacker snarled, throwing a punch. Blake ducked, then countered with a brutal jab to the ribs. The man grunted, staggering, but he recovered too quickly. Trained. Blake didn't have time for a prolonged fight. He needed an opening. A blur of movement to his right.

I scrambled across the floor and grabbed the gun. "Lane, don't—" Blake shouted.

I pulled the trigger. The bullet hit the attacker's shoulder, sending him to his knees with a pained yell. Blake yanked the gun from my grip before I could fire again. His breathing was rough and fast.

I was shaking. "I ... I had to—"

Blake grabbed my face, forcing me to look at him. "You did good," he said. "But we're not done yet."

He turned back to the attacker, but the man was already making his move. Bloodied but determined, he bolted toward an emergency exit.

Blake swore. "Stay here."

Then he was running, leaving me standing in the emptied hall. I collapsed on a chair, catching my breath. The conference center looked like the morning after an insane party. Chairs were tossed around like a tsunami had crashed through. Displays were destroyed; monitors black or displaying random pictures rather than their slick sales presentations. Flyers, promotional materials and swag were scattered all over the floor like New Year's confetti.

My eyes kept circling back to the door where Blake had disappeared chasing the mystery assailant. I was getting more nervous the longer he was missing. He had been such a constant and then with the kiss stirring up all kinds of questions, I was on the verge of tracking him down to make sure he wasn't hurt when he came striding through the door.

I jumped up and rushed over, seeing his pristine suit now dirtied. At least I didn't see any blood.

Blake's eyes were hard, his jaw tight. "We need to go. Now."

"Who was that guy?" I asked, falling into step next to him.

"I sent his picture to Sierra, but he suicided. We may never know." Blake growled.

"What?" I stuttered, shocked over the idea someone would kill themselves rather than be caught or talk.

"He told me this may be more about me than you." Blake said, around gritted teeth.

"I don't understand." I said, "What do you think that means?"

"Not here." Blake said, leading us down to the parking area.

Chapter 11
Under Attack
Blake Carter

We reached a black SUV. I hotwired it in seconds, the engine roaring to life.

Avery slid into the passenger seat. "Where are we going?"

My jaw clenched. "To end this."

She exhaled. "How?"

I glanced at her. "By finding out who's really behind it."

Avery met my gaze. She seemed to want to challenge me. I didn't blame her. We had been swimming against the current this whole time without any idea who was doing things. Then she nodded. I drove fast, weaving through the city streets with the kind of mindless precision that came from years of training. Avery sat beside me, gripping the armrest. By the way she chewed the inside of her cheek, and her eyes kept darting aimlessly, she was furiously thinking. Everything had spiraled. What had started as a possible corporate threat had turned into a full-blown war.

I glanced at her. "We need to lay low until we figure out our next move."

Avery exhaled. "And where exactly do we do that? Everywhere I go, they come after me."

I smirked. "I've got a place."

Avery rolled her eyes. "Of course you do."

Minutes later, we pulled into an unmarked warehouse on the outskirts of the city. I keyed in a code, the massive metal door groaning as it slid open. Inside was a fully equipped safe house. Weapons. Surveillance monitors. A secure server. This one was actually my own. Possibly unknown to even Sierra Bravo. I had never let anyone in here before. But, for Avery, I would break all the rules.

"What letter of the Sierra alphabet are we up to now?" she snarked.

"This is mine." I said quietly as I activated the systems.

Avery blinked. "You live like this?"

I shrugged. "I plan ahead."

She crossed her arms. "Paranoid much?"

I smirked. "Let's call it prepared."

I wasted no time. I pulled off the suit coat and tie and got to work. I moved to the surveillance desk, pulling up live feeds and encrypted files. Avery watched me, arms still folded.

"You really think this is more than someone wanting me?"

I didn't look up. "I don't think. I know."

Avery hesitated. "And if you're right?"

My jaw tightened. "Then someone wants both of us dead."

Silence stretched between us.

Then Avery pulled a chair beside me. "Okay. Let's find them first."

I glanced at her, assessing. She had changed, become a partner in this. Then I nodded. And together, we got to work. Hours passed. I analyzed data, tracking the sources of the threats, looking for patterns. Avery used her access to cross-check financial records and dig deep into corporate files. I quickly learned that she was not a tech CEO by accident. She had major skills at infiltrating supposedly secure computer networks. Slowly, a pattern emerged.

My voice was quiet. "Someone inside your company is funneling information to an external group."

Avery's frowned. "Someone I trusted."

I met her gaze. "Yeah."

Avery exhaled, rubbing her temples. "It never ends, does it?"

I hesitated. I wanted to reassure her, make it all okay. But Avery deserved the truth. I added softly, "Not until we end it."

Avery looked at me. For once, she seemed to believe me and had no argument.

Later that night, we took a break to rest our eyes and brains. We took drinks up to the rooftop of the warehouse. I set out lounge chairs for us to have a view of the city stretching before us. Avery pulled her jacket tighter around her shoulders.

"I used to love looking over the city." She said into the quiet darkness.

I glanced at her. "Used to?"

She sighed. "Now it feels like a battlefield with hidden snipers."

I stayed quiet for a moment. Funny. That's the way it always looked to me.

"Tell me something, Lane."

Avery arched a brow. 'What?"

My gaze didn't waver. "Why do you keep fighting?"

Avery swallowed. "Because if I don't, they win, and I won't let them."

I nodded slowly. "Yeah. I get that."

Avery studied me. "And what about you? Why do you fight?"

I exhaled. "Because I don't know how to do anything else."

The honesty made her look away. For the first time, she saw past the soldier, past the bodyguard. She saw *me*. I think it terrified her. Being that honest certainly rattled me. Before she could speak, my phone vibrated. A single message.

Not everyone you trust is who they seem.

My stomach dropped. I was sick of this cryptic shadow play.

Avery frowned. "What is it?"

I clenched my jaw. "Just another problem."

Avery stiffened. "What?"

I turned to her, my expression grim. "Nothing new. They say we're being betrayed from the inside."

I stared at the message, my grip tightening on the phone. I wanted to find out who this was so bad it was ripping a hole in my guts. I had spent years surviving in war zones, tracking enemies who hid behind false loyalties. But this? This was personal. Someone within our trusted circle was feeding the true enemy. And Avery wouldn't be safe until we cast light on the shadows and discovered who was behind this. I desperately wanted her to be safe.

Avery leaned closer, reading the message over my shoulder. "Not everyone you trust is who they seem," she murmured. She paused and then asked quietly "Do you think it's one of my board members?"

I exhaled sharply. "Could be. But it could also be someone in my network."

Avery's brows furrowed. "Your network?"

I hesitated not wanting to own up to starting to wonder about my own people. "I've got people I rely on. Contacts. Old friends. But in this business, trust can be a liability."

Avery folded her arms. "So, we're both surrounded by people who could be stabbing us in the back?"

I smirked. "Welcome to my world."

Avery's lips twitched, but the humor didn't reach her eyes.

"How do we figure out who it is?" she asked the skyline.

My expression hardened. "The problem of the hour. The only way to catch a rat is with a trap."

We went back downstairs and started brainstorming ideas. Most were ridiculous. Some put too much risk on Avery for me to even entertain. After too much coffee and no sleep, we came up with something we agreed on. The next morning, we put our plan into motion.

I had Connor, Sierra Bravo's tech genius, put false information on Avery's calendar. It was an encrypted file with fabricated details about a fake investor's meeting Avery was supposed to attend. The goal was simple: see who took the bait to come after her. I didn't like it, but Avery was right. She was the only reason that people would come out of hiding and make themselves known. She was the one who had to be out there tempting fate. I was going to get an ulcer on this job. If the mole was feeding the enemy as we assumed, the trap would spring itself. And I would be there to snap the jaws closed before anything could happen to Avery. I'd make damn sure of that.

Now, all we had to do was wait and that was the hardest part. By midday, I was restless. I didn't like playing defense. I was a man of action, built for battle, trained to strike before being struck. But this war required patience. Patience had never been my strong suit.

Avery paced the safe house, arms crossed. "Do you think it'll work?"

I ran a hand over my jaw. "If it doesn't, we rebait the trap with something more enticing."

She sighed, rubbing her temples. "I hate this."

I smirked. "Losing control?"

Her glare was half-hearted. "Don't push me, Carter."

I chuckled. "I wouldn't dare."

But even as I joked, I couldn't shake the feeling in my gut. Something was coming. I wasn't sure we were ready for it.

That evening, the trap snapped shut. One of the internal security alerts Avery had programmed pinged. A data transfer, straight from our planted file.

My eyes darkened as I hissed. "We got him."

Avery's breath caught. "Who?"

I typed rapidly, tracing the signal. Then I froze.

Avery leaned over. "What? Who is it?"

I froze, my teeth clenching in disbelief. The name on the screen made my blood turn to ice because it wasn't just anyone. It was someone I never thought would betray me. Someone I had once trusted with my life. I had gone to him for help. I exhaled, my voice barely above a whisper.

"It's Hale." I whispered, the very admission ripping through me.

Avery frowned. "Your military contact?"

I nodded, my jaw tight. "Yeah."

Avery swallowed. "What does that mean?"

"It means this came closer than I thought."

Damn it. I should have known. When he didn't get back to me. When he didn't have any info when I first got together with him. Maybe he was the one who called in the ones who attacked me with the knife. Would he have gone that far? If he was pressured. If he was paid enough. My fist slammed down on the desk.

Avery asked, rather timidly. "What now?"

I turned to her. I reined in my anger. I didn't want to frighten her. My voice was steadier than my racing thoughts. "Now, I go hunting."

Hale had been one of the few people I had even a shred of trust with. If I was compromised, what did that mean for everything else? I stood, pacing the room. My muscles were taut, my jaw clenched. I was far from my usual calm, but I couldn't just sit still.

Finally, she said, "You don't want to believe it."

"I don't." I stopped, my hands on my hips. "But evidence doesn't lie."

Avery hesitated. "If he really betrayed you… would you hesitate to stop him?"

I looked at her then, probably still looking somewhat dangerous and scary because that's what I was feeling. "No."

Avery shivered. I had spent my life making hard choices. I wanted her to have no doubt that if it came to it, I would eliminate Hale without a second thought. She was the priority here and way more than as just a client. And yet, there was a flicker of something else beneath my hardened mask. Doubt. Regret. But he had crossed a line that should never be crossed and against Avery on top of that. I could regret later if it came to that. But now? He was dead to me.

Avery took a step closer. "Blake."

I exhaled. "If Hale's working against us, we need to figure out who and why because he wouldn't have come up with this on his own." I met her gaze "Then we cut the head off the snake."

Avery swallowed. "How do we do that?"

My smirk was grim. "We set another trap. Worked once, why not again?"

Avery nodded. The war wasn't over. It was just getting started but at least we had some advantage now. We weren't waiting in a foxhole for the next message bomb to land. Avery's eyes told me she was thinking.

"If Hale has been feeding someone information, we know our next move." She said meeting my eyes.

My eyes darkened. "Exactly. Which is why we make them think they're leading while we stay three steps ahead."

Avery inhaled sharply. "And if Hale or someone moves first?"

My voice was ice. "Then we end this before they get the chance."

The line had been drawn.

Chapter 12
The Unseen Enemy
Avery Lane

Now that we knew a name, with Connor's help, we dug deep into everything Hale had touched. We had his IP addresses, and we knew his methodology, his digital fingerprints. Connor was a wizard himself at tracing data streams and tracking veritable shadows through the networks. He worked with us, slowly at first and then the evidence burst into the light. Messages, money transfers, emails. Like it or not, it was all there.

As I stared at the evidence we had uncovered, any concept of control I thought I had evaporated from my grasp. Betrayals. Not just from a rival. Not from a faceless enemy. From people I had trusted. That Blake had trusted. My whole world was an illusion built on that tenuous concept, and it was crumbling into rubble.

Money left my company undoubtedly used to pay off people who tried to kill me. Direct messages flew between different people in my own organization to make the transfers and cover them up. Security people were involved. IT, secretaries, clerical staff, management. There wasn't a level in the corporation that I could point to and say definitely "they're innocent". I was nauseous. Some of it was more harmless, more benign neglect than outright illegal actions but there was enough of that to make me cover my face willing it all to go away.

Blake brought me a sandwich, and I pushed the plate away unable to think about putting anything in my stomach in the face of this.

"This can't be real." I muttered behind my hands.

Blake's voice was quiet but firm. "It is and you have to eat."

I looked up at him. "Then tell me why it feels like my whole world is falling apart."

Blake met my gaze. "Because it is."

My hands trembled as I scrolled through the files. Bank transfers. Encrypted messages. Details of every move I had made for the last six months. Someone had been watching me carefully and feeding that information to an outside enemy, identity as yet unknown.

Blake leaned over my shoulder, his presence steady. "We need to list out who else is involved."

I exhaled shakily, refusing the threatening tears. "And if it's someone I can't bear to lose?"

Blake's jaw tightened. "Then you have to prioritize the list and choose. Personally? I'd clean house. Run lean until you can staff dependable people."

I clenched my fists. "I hate this."

Blake's voice softened. "I know."

And for the first time, I let myself believe him. The tension between us hadn't faded. If anything, it had thickened, curling around us like smoke. The safe house was quiet, too quiet. Night had fallen, leaving us with nothing but shadows and the weight of everything unsaid.

I slumped on the edge of the bed, my fingers raking through my hair, the weight of the day pressing down on me like a physical force. The safe house was dimly lit, the only light coming from a single lamp in the corner, casting long shadows across the room. Outside, the night was thick and silent, a stark contrast to the storm raging inside me.

"I don't even know who to trust anymore," I muttered, my voice heavy with exhaustion and doubt.

The betrayal of my own staff felt like a knife twisting in my own back, and I couldn't shake the feeling that everyone was a suspect now. Every email, every meeting, every handshake. It all seemed tainted, a carefully crafted lie designed to undermine me.

Blake leaned casually against the doorframe, his broad shoulders filling the space, his presence a quiet anchor in the chaos. He hadn't said much since we'd uncovered the evidence earlier that day, but his silence wasn't uncomfortable. It was steady, like he was waiting for me to process it all. His dark eyes watched me intently, his expression unreadable, but there was something in his gaze, a flicker of understanding, maybe even empathy.

"You trust me," he said, his tone steady, almost a challenge. His voice was low, rough around the edges, like gravel and velvet all at once. It was a voice that could command a room, but right now, it was just for me.

I glanced up, meeting his gaze, and immediately wished I hadn't. There was too much there, too much intensity, too much something. The words slipped out before I could stop them, not because I doubted him, but because I was drowning in uncertainty. "Do I?"

He didn't flinch. His eyes held mine, unwavering, like he was daring me to look away. "Yeah," he replied, his voice firm, like he was stating a fact. There was no arrogance in it, just a quiet confidence that made my chest tighten.

And in that moment, the realization hit me. Maybe that was the scariest part. Trusting him felt inevitable, but it also felt like stepping into uncharted territory, vulnerable and exposed. Blake wasn't just another colleague or ally; he was... more. I didn't know how to define it, and that terrified me.

I lay awake, staring at the ceiling, listening to the faint sound of Blake shifting in the chair across the room.

"Blake," I murmured.

He was silent for a moment. Then, "Yeah?"

I swallowed. "Do you ever wish things were different?"

Blake exhaled. "Every damn day."

Something about his voice made my chest ache.

Slowly, I sat up. "Then why do you keep fighting?"

Blake's gaze locked onto mine. "Because if I don't, I lose everything."

My throat tightened. "And what happens if you lose me?"

Blake didn't answer. But he didn't need to. I didn't realize I was moving until I was already standing, my feet carrying me across the room before I could second-guess myself. The safe house was quiet, the only sound the faint hum of the heater struggling against the autumn chill. Outside, the trees swayed in the wind, their shadows dancing on the walls like silent spectators. Blake remained still, his broad shoulders squared, his gaze locking onto mine as I stopped in front of him.

His presence filled the space, commanding and unyielding, just as it always had. But tonight, there was something different. The air between us crackled with an energy I couldn't ignore, a tension that had been building for days. It was in the way he looked at me when he thought I wasn't watching, in the way his hand lingered a fraction too long on my arm when he guided me through a crowd. It was in the kiss we'd shared, a stolen moment that had left me breathless and aching for more.

My heart hammered in my chest, a relentless rhythm that drowned out every rational thought. I should have turned around. Should have walked away and pretended this tension didn't exist. But I was done pretending. The threats against my life, the attempts on my life, they had stripped away the layers of pretense, leaving only raw, unfiltered truth. And the truth was, I wanted him. Desperately.

"Blake," I breathed, my voice trembling. The safe house felt smaller now, the walls closing in as if to bear witness to what was unfolding between us.

His chest rose sharply, his hands balling into fists at his sides.

"Don't," he warned, his tone low and strained.

His voice was gravel and steel, a sound that both soothed and terrified me. He was my bodyguard, my protector, but in this moment, he felt like something more, something dangerous and irresistible.

I ignored the warning, stepping closer. The scent of him reached me, soap and something distinctly masculine, a scent I'd come to associate with safety. But now, it made my pulse quicken for entirely different reasons.

"Tell me you don't feel it," I whispered, my voice barely a thread. "Tell me this doesn't matter."

Blake's jaw clenched, his eyes darkening as they held mine. They were a storm brewing, a mix of frustration, desire, and something else I couldn't name.

"It can't," he said, his voice rough. "It can't matter, Lane. Not like this."

I swallowed hard, my throat tight. "Why?" The word was a plea, a challenge, a question I wasn't sure I wanted answered.

His gaze burned into me, intense and unyielding. "Because I'm here to protect you. That's the job."

Was he trying to convince me? Or himself? I shook my head, my fingers curling into the fabric of my dress. It was a simple black sheath, something I'd chosen because it was practical, because it made me feel in control. But now, it felt like a barrier, a reminder of the distance he was trying to maintain.

"That's not all it is," I said, my voice steady despite the turmoil inside me.

Blake let out a ragged breath, his control slipping. "Damn it, Lane," he muttered, his hands flexing at his sides. "You don't know what you're asking."

I did know. I knew exactly what I was asking. I was asking him to see me, not just as his client, not just as a woman who needed protecting, but as a woman who wanted him. Who needed him in a way that had nothing to do with duty and everything to do with desire. Before I could respond, he moved.

One moment, there was space between us. The next, his hands were tangled in my hair, his lips crashing down on mine with a ferocity that stole my breath. His kiss was raw, desperate, a battle between restraint and need. His mouth was firm, demanding, his tongue sweeping into my mouth as if he'd been starving for this, for me, for far too long.

I gasped, my fingers digging into his shirt, pulling him closer. The fabric was rough against my palms, a stark contrast to the smoothness of his skin where it peeked through the open collar. His kiss was a storm, wild and unrelenting, and I was drowning in it, willingly, eagerly.

I knew we should stop. Knew this was reckless, dangerous. The threats against my life were real, and the last thing either of us needed was to blur the lines between professional and personal. But in that moment, nothing else mattered. The danger, the consequences, the rules? They all faded into the background, leaving only him and me and the hunger that had been simmering between us for far too long.

His hands moved, one sliding down my back to pull me tighter against him, the other cupping my jaw, his thumb brushing my cheekbone. His touch was firm but gentle, a stark contrast to the urgency of his kiss. I could feel the heat of him, the strength of him, the way his body seemed to fit perfectly against mine.

I moaned softly, my lips parting further, inviting him deeper. His taste was intoxicating, a mix of coffee and something uniquely him, something that made my knees weak and my heart race. His hand in my hair tightened, just enough to tug, and I shivered, my body responding to the roughness of his touch.

"Avery," he growled against my lips, his voice thick with need. "We shouldn't—"

I cut him off with another kiss, pressing myself against him, my breasts flush against his chest, my hips instinctively rocking into his.

"I don't care," I whispered when I finally pulled back, my breath coming in short, shallow gasps. "I don't care about the rules, about the danger. I just ... I need you, Blake. Right now. I need this."

His eyes searched mine, his expression a mix of longing and conflict. For a moment, I thought he might pull away, might retreat back into the role of my protector, the man who kept his distance, who kept his emotions in check. But then his gaze dropped to my lips, and something in him seemed to snap.

"Shit," he muttered, his hands moving to my waist, lifting me as if I weighed nothing.

I wrapped my legs around him instinctively, my arms tightening around his neck as he carried me toward the bed. He set me down gently, his lips never leaving mine, his hands never stopping their exploration. His kisses were hungry, possessive, as if he was trying to claim me, to make up for all the times he'd held back. I responded in kind, my fingers threading through his hair, my body arching into his as if I could get close enough to melt into him.

His hands moved to the hem of my dress, tugging it up without breaking our kiss. I lifted my hips to help him, the fabric sliding up my thighs, baring my skin to his touch. His hands were warm, calloused, as they slid up my legs, his thumbs brushing the lace of my panties. I shivered, my breath hitching as he paused, his lips trailing down my jaw, my neck, his teeth grazing my skin in a way that made me arch into him, a soft moan escaping my lips.

"You have no idea what you do to me," he murmured, his breath hot against my ear. His hands moved higher, his fingers hooking into the waistband of my panties, tugging them down slowly, deliberately. I lifted my hips, the fabric sliding down my legs, pooling at my feet.

I was bare to him now, exposed, and the vulnerability should have scared me. But with Blake, it didn't. With him, I felt safe, even as my heart pounded with anticipation, even as my body trembled with need.

His hands moved back to my waist, his lips finding mine again as he laid me down on the bed. The mattress was soft beneath me, a stark contrast to the hardness of his body as he loomed over me. His weight was a comfort, a promise, and I reached for him, my hands sliding under his shirt, my fingers tracing the muscles of his back.

He broke the kiss, his forehead resting against mine, his breath coming in ragged gasps. "Avery," he said, his voice a hoarse whisper. "Are you sure? Because once we start, there's no going back."

I smiled, my fingers curling into the skin of his back. "I've never been more sure of anything in my life," I said, my voice steady despite the storm raging inside me.

He kissed me again, softer this time, sweeter, as if he was trying to convey everything he couldn't say. Then, with a growl, he sat back, his hands moving to his belt, his eyes never leaving mine.

I watched, my heart pounding, as he undid his belt, his pants, revealing the hard length of him, already straining against his boxers. My breath caught, my body aching with anticipation, with need.

"You're killing me," he muttered, his hands moving to his boxers, tugging them down just enough to free himself.

I reached for him, my fingers wrapping around his shaft, my thumb brushing the tip. He hissed, his head falling back, his hands gripping my wrists as if to stop me, to hold me back. But I didn't stop. I stroked him slowly, deliberately, my touch firm but gentle, my eyes never leaving his.

"Avery," he groaned, his control slipping. "You're going to make me lose it."

I smiled, my other hand moving to his chest, my fingers tracing the lines of his muscles.

"Then lose it," I said, my voice a challenge, a promise. "Lose it with me."

His eyes burned into mine, his expression raw, unguarded. Then, with a growl, he leaned down, his lips capturing mine in a kiss that was both tender and fierce. His hands moved, one sliding down my body, his fingers brushing the wetness between my legs, the other tangling in my hair, holding me in place as he kissed me, deeper, harder, as if he was trying to pour every ounce of his desire into that one moment.

I moaned, my hips lifting into his touch, my body arching into his. His fingers slipped inside me, his thumb brushing my clit, and I gasped, my head falling back, my hands gripping his shoulders.

"Blake," I whispered, my voice a plea, a demand. "I need you. Now."

He pulled back, his eyes dark with desire, his breath coming in short, shallow gasps. "Tell me again," he said, his voice rough. "Tell me you want this. Tell me you want me."

I reached for him, my hands pulling him down, my lips finding his. "I want you," I murmured against his mouth. "I want you. Take me, Blake. Take me hard. Take me now."

His eyes flared, his control shattering. With a growl, he positioned himself between my legs, his hands gripping my hips as he thrust into me, filling me completely, his name a ragged whisper on my lips.

The bed creaked beneath us, the world narrowing to just the two of us, to the feel of him inside me, to the way his body moved against mine. His thrusts were deep, relentless, each one driving me closer to the edge. I met him stroke for stroke, my nails digging into his back, my legs wrapping around his waist as I clung to him, as I lost myself in him.

"Avery," he groaned, his voice thick with need. "Fuck, you feel so good."

I smiled, my lips finding his, my hands tangling in his hair. "Not as good as you," I whispered, my voice a breathless promise.

His kisses were hungry, possessive, his hands moving to my breasts, his thumbs brushing my nipples as he thrust into me, harder, faster, each stroke pushing me closer to the edge. I could feel it building, a coil tightening in my core, a tension that was both sweet and unbearable.

"Blake," I gasped, my body arching into his, my voice a plea. "I'm close. So close."

His eyes locked onto mine, his expression intense, unyielding. "Come for me," he growled, his voice, a command. "Come, Avery. Let me feel it."

His words were my undoing. With a cry, I shattered, my body convulsing around him, my nails digging into his back as wave after wave of pleasure washed over me. He followed, his thrusts stuttering, his name a hoarse whisper on my lips as he came, his body trembling as he spilled himself inside me.

For a moment, we stayed like that, our bodies still joined, our breaths coming in ragged gasps. Then, slowly, he pulled out, his hands moving to my hair, his lips brushing my forehead.

"Avery," he murmured, his voice soft, tender. "What the hell have we done?"

I smiled, my fingers tracing the lines of his face. "I'm not sure," I said, my voice steady despite the storm of emotions raging inside me. "But I'm not sorry."

He kissed me, softly this time, sweetly, tenderly. Then, with a sigh, he sat up, his hands moving to his clothes, his expression distant, thoughtful.

I watched him, my heart pounding, my mind racing. What had we done? What did this mean? The threats against my life, the danger, it was still there, lurking in the shadows, waiting for the right moment to strike.

But in that moment, none of it mattered. Right now, all that mattered was him, was us, was the way his hand found mine, his fingers lacing through mine as if to say, without words, that whatever came next, we'd face it together.

The night was far from over, and the dawn would bring its own challenges. But for now, in the quiet of the safe house, with Blake by my side, I felt something I hadn't felt in a long time: hope. And maybe, just maybe, that was enough. Blake pulled away first.

His breathing was uneven, his hands still tangled in my hair. "We can't."

My heart pounded. 'You keep saying that, but you're still here."

Blake let out a bitter chuckle. "That's the problem."

I exhaled. "Then tell me what we do now."

He hesitated. Then, finally, he said, "We end this cat and mouse game. We make sure you're safe."

I nodded. Whatever this was between us, it had to wait. For now.

We dressed and returned to the files. The deeper we dug, the worse it got. More names. More secrets. More proof that the enemy wasn't just outside. They were inside.

I clenched my fists. "I want to burn them all down."

Blake smirked. "Now you're thinking like me."

I exhaled. "How do we figure out who's pulling the strings?"

Blake's expression hardened. "We wait for them to slip up."

I crossed my arms. "And if they don't?"

Blake's voice was cold. "Then we make them."

Hours later, the breakthrough came. Yet another message. Coded. Encrypted. But not enough to stop us. Connor cracked it within minutes. Blake's expression darkened as he read.

My stomach twisted waiting for the next nonsense words. "What does it say?"

Blake turned to me; his voice grim. "It says we've been looking at the wrong person."

My pulse spiked. "What do they mean?"

Blake exhaled. "It means the real mastermind..." He met my gaze. "...is someone we never suspected." My blood ran cold but my temper was hot. Did this mean the enemy had been in plain sight all along? Then now, it was time to bring them all down.

Blake grabbed the phone from my hands, scanning a new message. His jaw tensed. "They're taunting us."

I exhaled sharply. "Or warning us."

Blake's voice was cold. "Same thing."

My mind raced. "Maybe it means they know we're close. Whoever's behind this, they've been watching our every move."

Blake ran a hand through his hair. "Then we need to move faster."

I stared at the message again. A knot formed in my stomach. I was never supposed to find out. Someone had expected me to stay blind. To never question. To never look too deep. Someone I had trusted.

My throat tightened. "What if I already know who it is?"

Blake's gaze sharpened. "Say it."

I hesitated. Then, my voice barely above a whisper— "My CFO, Roger Whitman."

Blake frowned. "You sure?"

I swallowed hard. "No."

But in my gut, it felt right. I sat on the couch stewing, debating back and forth on whether it could be Roger. Blake moved with precision, doing something more with security measures. I had spent years building walls. Keeping people out. And now, one of the few people I had let in had apparently betrayed me.

Blake sat beside me. "We're going to take him down, Lane."

I met his gaze. "How?"

Blake's lips curled into a smirk. "We let him think he's won."

I arched a brow. "Another trap?"

Blake nodded. "We give him what he wants. Make him feel safe. And when he makes his move?"

My breath hitched. "We take everything from him."

Blake's smirk deepened. "You're getting pretty good at thinking like me."

I exhaled, shaking my head. "That's terrifying."

Blake chuckled. "You'll get used to it."

The plan was set. I would act like nothing had changed. I'd return to the office, pretend to be shaken but unaware of the betrayal. Meanwhile, Blake would stay at my side and Connor would track every digital move Roger made. Having a plan didn't diminish the tension. I sat on the edge of the bed in the safe house, staring at the floor. Blake leaned against the doorway.

"You should rest," he said.

I shook my head. "Can't."

Blake hesitated, then walked over, sitting beside me. For a long moment, neither of us spoke.

Then, softly, I asked, "What if we don't win?"

Blake exhaled. "Then we go down swinging."

I looked at him. Suddenly, nothing felt more terrifying than losing him. I turned toward him, my fingers brushing his. Blake didn't pull away. Instead, he laced his fingers with mine. No words. Just silent understanding. Morning came after an impossibly long night.

Blake was already up, checking the security feeds, coffee made. I pulled myself together, slipping back into the role of CEO, the one who had everything under control. But deep down, I knew. That was the biggest pretense of all. Everything was about to change. Then Blake's phone buzzed. I was starting to hate our phones.

Another message. Coded. Encrypted. Blake frowned, working fast to decode it. A moment later, his body tensed.

I stepped closer. "What is it?"

Blake turned to me, his expression unreadable. Then, finally, he spoke.

"We *have* been looking in the wrong place."

My pulse quickened. "What do you mean?"

Blake's voice was grim. "The mastermind?"

He turned the screen toward me. My breath caught. Because staring back at me was a name I never expected. Someone even closer than

Roger. Someone I never saw coming. And just like that— my world shattered. My knees felt weak.

I gripped the edge of the desk, my breath unsteady. The name on the screen blurred as my mind tried to reject what was right in front of me.

Blake watched me carefully. "Lane—"

I shook my head. "No. It can't be."

Blake's voice was calm but firm. "It is."

I swallowed hard. "I trust ... trusted him."

Blake's jaw tightened. "I know."

Silence stretched between us, thick with betrayal, disbelief. Finally, I straightened. My voice was steady.

"Then we finish this."

Blake nodded. And in that moment, there was no hesitation. No fear. Only war. Me and my soldier. I was ready to destroy them all.

Blake's jaw tightened. 'No more running."

I met his gaze. "No more waiting."

It was time to strike first.

Chapter 13
Reckless Decisions

Avery Lane

My pulse pounded as I stared at the blueprint Blake had spread out on the table. The dim glow of the laptop screen cast sharp shadows across the war room, a makeshift setup in his safe house, where we had spent the last eight hours unraveling the tangled web of threats against my company. Every second counted. Blake tapped the blueprint with two fingers.

"This is the best entry point. If they're coming for you and they will, this is where they'll strike."

I exhaled sharply, rubbing my temples. The weight of the past week had drained me, but I couldn't afford to show weakness. I just had to keep going for a little while longer. At least that's what I kept telling myself.

"Should we call the authorities?" I asked.

I already knew what Blake's response would be.

Blake's jaw tightened. "No. We don't know who we can trust. Someone on the inside is feeding information to unknown parties and they have a lot of money riding on this. Enough that I don't trust even those sworn to protect and serve, sadly."

The truth burned in my gut. We knew the CFO was at least partially responsible for the attempts on my life. If we made the wrong move, it could cost everything. I met Blake's eyes, searching for certainty in the storm of doubt raging inside me.

"Then what do we do?"

Blake leaned in, his voice low and steady. "We are setting a trap."

I had always prided myself on being rational, on weighing risks before making decisions. But tonight, rationality warred with desperation. I knew Blake's plan was dangerous, reckless, but I also knew we were running out of options. My fingers tightened around the edge of the marble countertop. And this situation was more his area of expertise than mine. I had to trust him. And, God help me, I did.

"Let's go over it." Blake nodded, unfolding the map. "The attack will come when you're most vulnerable, in a setting where they think security is stretched thin. This makes tomorrow's gala reception for Vanguard's premier level investors as the best venue we could ask for. The place has a lot of access and there will be a ton of media there to capture the event. If they want to publicly bring you down, where better? Security would be hard-pressed to keep track of everything, or so most would think. The place is huge. That sounds like a bad thing, but it is open. Perfect for us. With that event, they are going to expect us to be caught off guard, unable to do much."

My breath hitched. "And instead?"

"We will have total control of the battlefield." Blake's voice was pure steel. "I'll position my team strategically, monitoring every entrance, every exit, every window. There will be walk through metal detectors. The media and catering staff have already been vetted and there will be no one allowed in who is a last-minute replacement. Several team members will be acting as undercover guests inside the ballroom. The moment anyone makes a move, we shut them down."

I hesitated. "And if they come at me directly?"

Blake's eyes darkened. "Then I'll be there right by your side."

It wasn't the words. It was the way Blake said them, with unwavering conviction. The way his body was coiled like a spring, ready to strike. The way he looked at me like I was something precious, something worth protecting at any cost.

I swallowed. "Okay."

By the time midnight arrived, the plan was set. We worked in tense silence, refining every contingency, every fallback. Blake spent half his time on the phone, getting Connor set up, relaying instructions to his team. It felt like we were preparing for an incursion into enemy territory. Maybe we were. At some point, Blake disappeared into the adjoining room, leaving me alone with my ragged thoughts. I exhaled slowly, glancing at the city skyline beyond the windows. The weight of the night settled over my shoulders. A sound behind me made me turn.

Blake stood in the doorway, arms crossed. "You should get some rest."

I let out a hollow laugh. "Sleep isn't exactly an option right now."

Blake stepped closer. "I know you're scared."

I didn't deny it. "I hate feeling this way. Like I have no control."

Blake's gaze softened. "You're not alone in this."

For a moment, the space between us shrunk. I could hear the steady rhythm of Blake's breathing, could feel the warmth of his presence. It wasn't fear that made my pulse quicken. I looked away first. "I only have to worry about our plan for the gala."

"That's the spirit. " Blake offered his smirk.

The next morning, I sat in my office, pretending to work while my mind raced in neutral unable to focus on anything. The gala was hours away. If we were right, whoever was behind the attacks would make their move tonight. A soft knock sounded at my door. I looked up, my heart skipping. It was Roger Whitman, my CFO.

"Hey," he said, stepping inside. "You okay? You've been tense this morning."

I forced a smile. "Just a lot on my mind. Big night."

Roger studied me. "If something's wrong, you can tell me. You know, right?"

Last week, I would have agreed with him, and I wanted to believe him. But evidence had piled up, and I couldn't ignore it.

"I appreciate that, Roger. Really."

He nodded but didn't push. "I'll see you at the gala."

As he walked out, a chill ran down my spine and I put my head in my hands. Tonight, I had to be prepared for someone to betray me. Anyone want to be me for a day? I want to go home and go to bed. Preferably with my bodyguard. I need therapy.

To the outside world, I was a CEO hosting a lavish event. my demeanor polished and composed. In reality, I was walking into a battlefield. My eyes were looking everywhere, waiting for something to jump out at me. Blake stayed close, his sharp gaze scanning the crowd. I lifted a champagne flute to my lips, scanning the room for any sign of danger. I don't why I bothered. He would see it long before I did but I couldn't help myself. Every face felt like a threat. Every movement seemed suspicious.

The gala was a whirlwind of flashing cameras, glittering gowns, and murmured conversations. I played my part, smiling and shaking hands, but my pulse pounded with anticipation. Blake was never more than a few feet away, his presence grounding me, an anchor in a storm, an anchor I had never needed before but now clung to like a life preserver. He moved like a shadow, scanning the crowd with a quiet intensity that sent a clear message: nothing would happen to me with him on watch.

Then, I spotted him. Ethan Graves. My breath caught. I hadn't seen him in years. We dated. I ended it. He disagreed and started stalking me. It turned violent. I put him behind bars for that. And here he was, standing at the edge of the ballroom, watching me with a smirk that sent ice through my veins.

"Blake," I whispered.

Blake knew who he was from when we had dissected my past. I hadn't spent a lot of time discussing Ethan, but he did classify as a potential enemy; so, he made Blake's initial list. Blake followed my gaze, and I didn't miss the way his entire body tensed.

"I'll handle this," Blake said, already moving.

"No," I said urgently. "It might just be a distraction—"

But before I could say another word, the lights cut out. Screams erupted as the entire ballroom was plunged into darkness. My heartbeat thundered in my chest. I barely had time to react before strong arms wrapped around me, yanking me backwards. I struggled, but my captor was too forceful. A sharp sting at my neck. My brain leapt. I'd been injected with something. Panic surged as my limbs turned to lead. Blake— The last thing I saw was a familiar face, twisted in betrayal. Then, darkness.

Chapter 14
The Rescue Mission
Blake Carter

My knuckles tightened around the steering wheel as I navigated the darkened streets at breakneck speed. My mind raced even faster, calculating every possible scenario, every potential risk. Avery was out there, taken. The thought alone sent a bolt of fury through my veins. I had one job, one damn job: to keep her safe. And I'd failed. I'd fallen for a distraction. One of the oldest tricks and there I went.

I forced my emotions into submission. Panic wouldn't save Avery. Precision, strategy, and sheer willpower would. I tapped the earpiece nestled against my ear. "Connor, tell me you've got a location."

"Triangulating," Connor's voice crackled through the line. "They're smart, using encrypted channels, but I've got a ping on an abandoned warehouse on the outskirts of the city. Looks like a good place for a hostage situation."

My jaw clenched. "Send me the coordinates. I'm going in."

"You should wait for backup. They're six minutes behind you."

"Not an option."

I killed the connection, my pulse a steady drumbeat in my ears. Backup meant delay, and delay meant danger. Every second Avery remained in their hands was another second, she was at risk. I wouldn't give them that.

The warehouse loomed ahead, a skeletal structure of rusted metal and shattered windows. I parked half a mile away, slipping out of the vehicle with practiced ease. The cold night air bit at my skin, but I welcomed the sharpness. It kept me grounded.

I moved like a shadow, hugging the darkness, my instincts acute. The building had one obvious entrance, but conspicuous meant expected. I scanned the perimeter, spotting a side window half boarded up. That was my way in.

I pulled a knife from my tactical vest, sliding it beneath the wooden slats. A quiet pop, and I had enough space to slip through. I landed softly inside, crouched low. The air was thick with oil and rust, the distant hum of some fan was the only sound. My grip tightened around my weapon. I desperately needed eyes on Avery.

Connor's voice filtered through my earpiece. "Drone confirms heat signatures for multiple hostiles. Looks like someone's restrained in a main room, northeast quadrant."

My muscles coiled. "Number of guards?"

"Four, possibly more. One stationed outside, the others inside. And I... there's someone else with her. Someone not moving away."

My stomach turned. If they'd hurt her ... I forced the thought down. It was clouding my judgement more than I could allow. No. I couldn't think that. I was already tamping down rage to function at all. My imagination would only get her killed.

"Keep me updated," I whispered, moving forward.

Every step was calculated. I stuck to the shadows, my movements controlled. The first guard was easy, an elbow to the throat, a swift takedown. No noise. No alarm raised.

I slid through the corridors, the dim lighting barely enough to see. Then I heard it: Avery's voice. I actually took a full breath. Not only alive but arguing. That's my girl!

"I don't know what you think you'll gain from this," She snapped. "Untie me and I won't put you in jail again."

A chuckle followed. A voice I recognized. Ethan Graves. The realization hit me like a freight train. Ethan, the ex, the traitor. The man she had put behind bars. And, he had Avery. My grip on my weapon tightened as I reached the door to the main room. I took a slow breath, steadying my pulse. I had to be smart. Rushing in would get us both killed. I peered through the crack in the door.

Avery sat in a chair, wrists bound to its arms, but defiant. Ethan stood in front of her, smirking, while two other men flanked the walls.

I counted three. Three men between me and Avery. I could take them. I moved. The door burst open, and before the nearest guard could react, my fist collided with his jaw, sending him sprawling. The second man lunged, but I was faster, twisting my arm and slamming him into the wall. A swift strike to the throat, and he dropped.

That left Ethan.

I leveled my gun. "Step away from her."

Ethan raised his hands, a smug grin stretching across his face. "Blake Carter. The wanna be hero."

"Untie her. Now."

Ethan didn't move. "You don't know why she's here, do you?"

My finger hovered over the trigger. I really wanted to pull it. "I don't care."

"You should." Ethan stepped closer. "Because this isn't about revenge. It's about justice."

My gut twisted. Justice?

"What the hell are you talking about?"

Ethan's grin widened. "Ask Avery."

My eyes flickered to her. For the first time, uncertainty swam in her gaze.

"Don't listen to him," she said. "He is a lying bully."

Ethan chuckled. "She's not as innocent as you think."

My mind warred between instinct and doubt. Then, before I could react—

A gunshot. Pain exploded through my shoulder. Avery screamed my name. The world tilted. Darkness closed in.

My vision blurred for a fraction of a second as the pain shot through my shoulder. I barely registered the warm trickle of blood soaking into my shirt before instinct took over. I rolled, using the momentum to avoid a second shot, and fired back.

A grunt. One of the guards went down. The other scrambled for cover, and Ethan took a step back, dragging Avery's chair with him. I saw the panic flicker in his eyes. Good. Fear made people reckless.

"Drop the gun, Carter," Ethan said, his smirk faltering. "Or I put a bullet in her next."

I steadied my breathing. I needed to think fast. My injury slowed me, but it wasn't enough to take me out of the fight. I had to create an opening. Keep Ethan talking.

"You've already lost," I said. "My team is outside. This place is surrounded."

Ethan's jaw twitched, but he covered it. "You're bluffing."

I shrugged, ignoring the sharp pain the movement caused. "Am I? You want to take that risk?"

A flicker of doubt. Then, a crashing sound from outside. A distraction. I didn't waste the opportunity. I lunged. Ethan's hand jerked as he fired. I twisted when I saw his movement, the bullet missing me by inches as I slammed into Ethan, knocking the gun from his grip. We hit the ground hard, grappling for control. My shoulder screamed in protest, but I didn't let up. This wasn't a fight. It was survival for both Avery and me.

Avery struggled against her restraints, her eyes locked on us, desperation and determination flickering across her face.

"Blake!" she shouted.

Ethan clawed at my wound, pressing down cruelly. Agony seared through me, but I used the pain, channeled it. Got angrier. With a surge of strength, I flipped Ethan over, pinning him. The fight wasn't over. Not yet. Ethan thrashed beneath me, fighting like a man with nothing to lose. I gritted my teeth, using my weight to keep him pinned, but the pain in my shoulder was making it harder to maintain control. Blood loss was slowing me down. I had to end this.

A movement in my periphery caught my attention. The remaining guard was recovering, reaching for his weapon.

I shifted my grip, twisting Ethan's arm behind my back. "You move, and I snap it."

The guard hesitated, his hand hovering over the gun.

"Do it," Ethan spat. "Shoot him!"

The hesitation lasted half a second too long. A loud *crack* echoed through the warehouse as I dislocated Ethan's shoulder. His scream tore through the air, and in the distraction, I kicked out, knocking the guard's weapon across the floor.

Avery seized the moment. With a sharp movement, she shifted her chair, slamming its wooden legs into the guard's shin. He stumbled, cursing, and before he could recover, I had him in a chokehold. Minutes later, the man went limp. I released him, my chest heaving. Ethan groaned beneath him, his face twisted in pain.

Connor's voice crackled in my earpiece. "Blake! I've got backup en route. ETA three minutes. What's your status?"

I wiped the sweat from my brow, forcing myself to focus. "Avery's secure. Target subdued. Send medics. Target needs one and I've been hit."

A soft gasp pulled my attention. Avery's eyes locked onto my wound, concern tightening her features. "You're bleeding."

I exhaled, the adrenaline still keeping the worst of the pain at bay. "It's not so bad."

She didn't believe me. I could see it in her eyes. Well, I *was* lying.

Avery struggled against her restraints, frustration flashing across her face. "Get me out of this."

I retrieved the knife from my vest, slicing through the ropes binding her wrists. The moment she was free, she lurched forward, her hands pressing against my wounded shoulder.

"You shouldn't be moving," she said, her voice unsteady but full of concern.

I let out a weak chuckle. "I could say the same to you."

She shook her head, her fingers tightening as she applied pressure to slow the bleeding. "I thought—"

She didn't finish the sentence, but she didn't have to. I could see it in her expression. The fear followed by the relief.

I reached up, brushing a stray lock of hair from her face. "I told you. I'm not going anywhere." I said softly.

For a moment, neither of us spoke. The weight of everything settled between us. The fear. The danger. The unspoken words hanging in the air. Then, movement. Ethan groaned, shifting. My attention snapped back to him, my instincts on high alert. The bastard was still conscious. And I was smiling. It was not a very nice smile.

Chapter 15
Breaking Point

Avery Lane

My wrists ached from the ropes that bound me, but I barely noticed. My mind was sharper than the pain, focused on the man pacing before me. Ethan Graves. His presence alone was enough to stoke the flames of fury and fear battling inside me. I had spent years convincing myself that he was gone and I'd never see him again. A mistake from the past, buried under the weight of time. But here he was, standing in front of me, very much here. And very much unhinged.

"You look different, Avery," Ethan mused, tilting his head as he studied me. "More polished. But I suppose money does that, doesn't it?"

It took all I had not to react. I wouldn't give him the satisfaction. "And you look desperate. What's the matter, Ethan? Prison not the redemption arc you were hoping for?"

His smirk flickered, the first crack in his carefully constructed façade. "You're still damn arrogant. That's always been your problem."

"My problem?" I forced out a short, humorless laugh. "Says the man who went from Wall Street golden boy to convicted felon." I needed him to think I was fearless, in control. Though God knew, both were lies. I was wide eyed and breathing frantically out of simply teeth gritting determination. I was banking on Blake being able to find me, to rescue me. Though using that word turned my stomach, it was what I desperately needed. I didn't trust Ethan not to hurt me or to take me somewhere far away where Blake would never find me. If I weren't tied, I would try to escape but there was nothing I could do currently.

Ethan's expression darkened. "You did this to me."

I wasn't sure what he meant by *this* but I'd play along. "You did it to yourself."

"Don't pretend you're innocent," Ethan snapped, stepping closer. "We built something together. You were supposed to be my partner, and you turned your back on me."

My chest tightened. The past had long since hardened with scar tissue, but Ethan's words threatened to tear it open again.

"You were stealing from our investors, Ethan. You were ruining lives."

He scoffed. "And yet, here you are, running your empire like you did it all on your own. Tell me, Avery, do you sleep soundly knowing your hands aren't as clean as you think?"

A chill crept down my spine. I clenched my fists, forcing my breathing to remain steady. "This isn't about business. You're obsessed. That's why I'm here."

Ethan's jaw tensed but he didn't deny it. The air between us thickened, a suffocating tension wrapping around my chest. I needed to keep him talking, needed to stall. Blake would come for me. I had to believe that. Otherwise, fear would crawl up my throat and choke me.

Ethan let out a slow exhale, shaking his head. "You don't get it, do you? It was never about business."

My pulse spiked, but I refused to look away. I asked in a bored tone. I had learned how to act courtesy of too many meetings with influential people. "Then what was it?"

Ethan's lips curled into something that wasn't a smile. "You. It was always you."

A shudder ran through me, a mix of disgust and dread. So, he was still obsessed about me, our relationship. I forced myself to keep my expression neutral. "That's not love, Ethan. It's control. You never had control over me."

His fingers twitched at his side. "I could have."

I swallowed hard. The depth of his delusion sent a sharp pulse of fear through me. He believed what he was saying. That was what made him dangerous. I needed to keep him talking. Whatever he had planned, I wanted no part in it. The door rattled so softly it was almost unheard. Both of us froze. Ethan turned sharply, his hand going to the gun at his hip. My heart pounded. Was it Blake? I needed to distract Ethan. Then. A crash. The door burst open, and the world exploded into chaos. Blake!

I barely had time to process it was really him before he was in the room, moving with lethal precision. A shot rang out. Ethan's gun fired wild. I did choke but it missed Blake by inches. In the next breath, Blake tackled him to the ground, knocking the weapon away.

I struggled against my restraints, panic surging as I watched them fight. Blood smeared across Blake's shoulder where he had already been wounded, but he didn't slow. Ethan clawed at Blake's injury, trying to weaken him, but Blake was faster. Stronger. A sickening *crack* echoed as Blake's fist connected with Ethan's jaw, sending him sprawling. He didn't get up. The room fell silent. Blake turned, his breathing heavy, his eyes locking onto mine. Relief hit me like a tidal wave. I blinked fast as my eyes grew wet.

My fingers trembled as Blake sliced through the ropes. The moment I was free, I threw myself forward, wrapping my arms around him just to make sure he was really here and okay. I felt the tension in his body, the hesitation but then, his arms closed around me, solid and unyielding.

"You're safe," Blake murmured, his voice rough.

"So are you." I echoed.

I buried my face against his good shoulder, my breath coming in shuddering waves. "I knew you'd come."

Blake pulled back, his hands framing my face. His thumb brushed over a bruise forming along my cheekbone, his jaw tightening. "Did he—"

"I'm okay," I whispered. "You got here in time."

His gaze searched mine, maybe making sure I was telling the truth. Then, ever so slowly, he nodded. His lips slowly descended onto mine and I melted into the kiss. Sirens wailed in the distance.

Connor sent in Sierra backup. A medic checked Blake's injury, but he waved them off, his focus on me. I felt the weight of everything crashing down at once. The fear. The adrenaline. The exhaustion. My knees wobbled, but before I could fall, Blake was there.

"I've got you," he murmured.

And I believed him. This nightmare was over.

Ethan stirred, groaning as he lifted himself off the floor. Blake was on him in an instant, pressing a knee into his back to keep him down. I inhaled sharply, my heart hammering as I took in the scene, Ethan's face twisted in fury, his hands curling into fists despite his clear disadvantage.

"This isn't over," Ethan spat, his voice thick with venom. "You think you've won?"

Blake didn't flinch. "You're done, Graves."

Ethan let out a bitter laugh. "You believe that?" His gaze flickered to me, dark and unreadable. "There's more at play here than you realize."

I forced myself to stand tall. I wouldn't let him see my fear. "Whatever you think you're fighting for, Ethan, it's over."

His expression shifted, something between amusement and pity. "You always were naïve."

Blake applied more pressure, making Ethan grunt in pain. "Shut up."

I exhaled shakily, my fingers still tingling from being tied up for too long. My body ached, my mind tried to process the idea of more threats, but one thought overpowered everything else, I was free. Blake had come for me.

"Avery."

I turned at the sound of my name, meeting Connor's concerned gaze as he came into the room. "Jeez, are you okay?"

I nodded automatically. "Yeah."

Connor's eyes flickered to Blake. "And you?"

Blake smirked, though it didn't reach his eyes. "I'll live."

Connor didn't seem convinced, but he let it go. Instead, he handed Blake a phone. "This came through a secure channel. You need to hear it."

Blake frowned, pressing the device to his ear. As the message played, his entire demeanor changed.

I stepped closer, sensing the shift. "What is it?"

Blake lowered the phone slowly, his jaw clenched. When he finally spoke, his voice was tight.

"There's another threat."

My stomach dropped. I had thought this was over. But it wasn't. I felt the weight of the words settle over me like a lead blanket. Another threat.

I clenched my fists. "What do you mean another threat?"

He hesitated, choosing his words carefully. "The message didn't give specifics, but it's not over. Someone was working with Ethan... they're still out there."

A chill ran down my spine. "So, this wasn't about just him."

Blake shook his head. "No. And until we know who's behind it, you're still in danger."

I swallowed hard. I was exhausted, emotionally drained, but there was no time to rest.

Blake met my gaze, his voice unwavering. "I'm not leaving your side."

I felt something deep inside me shift. I had spent a long time convincing myself that I didn't need anyone. That I could handle anything on my own. But standing here, with Blake, I realized, I didn't want to do this alone. And for the first time in a long time, I didn't have to.

Chapter 16
Healing and Recovery
Blake Carter

I had taken bullets before. I had survived explosions, brutal hand-to-hand combat, and nights spent in the dirt behind enemy lines. None of that compared to the exhaustion pressing down on me now. I had no idea when I had last slept. I sat in Avery's penthouse, an ice pack pressed against my injured shoulder. The city glittered beyond the floor-to-ceiling windows, an illusion of calm that didn't match the storm raging inside me.

Avery was sitting across from me, her fingers wrapped around a glass of wine she hadn't touched. Dark smudges shadowed her eyes, remnants of too many sleepless nights and too much stress. She was safe. I kept telling myself that. She was alive. But the weight in my chest refused to lift.

"You should get some rest," she murmured, breaking the silence.

I let out a quiet chuckle, shaking my head. "I could say the same to you."

She exhaled, rubbing her temples. "I don't even know where to start, Blake. My company's been dragged through the mud. Half my board wants me to take a leave of absence. The press won't stop speculating about what's happening. And on top of it all, I—"

Her voice wavered.

I leaned forward. "What?"

Her eyes met mine, bleak and hollow. Vulnerable. "I don't know how to feel about any of this."

Neither did I.

In the day since Avery's rescue, the world hadn't stopped moving. I had worked alongside Avery's team, trying to contain the damage. Vanguard, her revolutionary AI security program, was under scrutiny. Investors were panicking. Avery was fighting to keep control of her company. And through it all, I had been there. At first, it was strictly business, overseeing security, coordinating with law enforcement. But as the adrenaline faded, something else settled between us. An awareness. An understanding that neither of us could put into words.

I knew what it was. I just didn't know what to do with it.

We spent the next morning in Avery's office, poring over reports and proposed damage control strategies. I stood near the window, watching her as she read through legal documents, her expression tight with frustration.

"You're pushing yourself too hard," I said.

She didn't look up. "I don't have a choice."

"You always have a choice."

She let out a sharp breath, tossing the papers onto the desk. "You don't understand, Blake. This company, it's my life. If I lose control, I lose everything."

I crossed the room, stopping just beside her chair. "You almost lost your real life, Avery. That matters more than any company."

Silence.

Then, quietly, she whispered, "I don't know how to separate them."

I hesitated, then reached out, my fingers brushing against hers. "Maybe you don't have to do this alone."

Her gaze lifted, locking onto mine. The air between us grew heavy. Then, a knock at the door shattered the moment.

Connor walked in, somber "You need to see this."

Connor slid the tablet across the sleek glass table, his face etched with a grimness that mirrored the weight of the situation.

"It's another leak. Fresh." His voice was low, almost a whisper, but it carried the gravity of a bomb detonating in slow motion.

I watched as Avery's fingers trembled as she reached for it, her knuckles brushing against the cool surface. Her eyes darted across the screen, scanning the lines of text and data like a soldier reading a death sentence. The color drained from her face, leaving her complexion as pale as the afternoon light filtering through her office windows.

"This is internal," she murmured, her voice barely audible. "Company secrets. How—?"

I leaned forward, my elbows resting on the table, my jaw clenching hard enough to grind stone. "Where the hell did this come from?" The question hung in the air, heavy and unanswered.

Connor shook his head, his dark hair falling into his eyes as he rubbed his temples. "That's the kicker. No trail. Whoever did this, they're a ghost. Better than anything I've seen."

Avery's hands flew to her temples, her nails digging into her skin as if she could physically push away the panic rising in her chest.

"This is a disaster," she whispered, her voice shaking. "If this gets out—"

I cut her off, my voice steady, a lifeline in the storm. "It won't. We'll handle it."

Her eyes met mine, wide and searching, as if she were looking for something, anything, to hold onto. "How?"

I locked my gaze with hers, unyielding. "Together."

The word hung between us, a promise, a vow. Avery's breath hitched, and for a moment, the world seemed to pause. I could see the tension in her shoulders, the way her chest rose and fell with each ragged breath. I'd seen men crumble under less pressure. I wouldn't let her fall apart.

The meeting ended in silence, the three of us sitting quietly, the weight of the leak pressing down on us like a physical force. But as Connor excused himself, leaving Avery and me alone, the air shifted. The tension didn't dissipate. It transformed.

That night, Avery didn't retreat to the bedroom like she usually did. She didn't say a word, but when I settled beside her on the plush leather couch, she didn't flinch. My safe house was bathed in the soft glow of the city lights filtering through the bulletproof glass of the windows, casting a warm amber hue over everything. The air was thick with the scent of jasmine from the fresh flowers on the coffee table, mingling with the faint aroma of the red wine she'd been sipping earlier. It was as if the world outside, with its chaos, its threats, its relentless demands, had ceased to exist. Here, in this moment, there was only her and me.

Avery's hands were clasped tightly in her lap, her knuckles white. I reached out, my fingers brushing against hers, and she didn't pull away. Instead, she turned her palm up, her skin warm and soft against mine. I laced our fingers together, feeling the tremor in her hand, the vulnerability she tried so hard to hide.

"You're not alone in this," I said, my voice low and steady. "We'll figure it out. Together."

She nodded, but her eyes remained downcast, her lashes casting shadows on her cheeks. "I'm scared," she admitted, the words barely audible.

I squeezed her hand, pulling her closer until our shoulders touched. "It's okay to be scared. But we're not going to let this break us."

She finally looked up, her eyes meeting mine, and in that moment, something shifted. The fear was still there, but beneath it, I saw something else, a spark, a flicker of something raw and unguarded.

"What if we can't stop it?" she asked, her voice trembling.

"We will," I replied firmly. "Because we don't have a choice. And because..." I paused, my thumb brushing the back of her hand. "Because I won't let you face this alone."

Her breath caught, and for a long moment, we just sat there, our hands entwined, the weight of the world outside feeling impossibly distant. The silence between us was heavy, charged, electric.

Then, slowly, she leaned into me, her head resting on my shoulder. Her hair smelled like lavender and something uniquely her, a scent that always made my heart skip a beat. I wrapped my arm around her, pulling her closer, feeling the warmth of her body against mine.

"Thank you," she whispered, her voice muffled against my shirt.

"For what?"

"For being here. For not letting me fall apart."

I smiled, pressing a kiss to the top of her head. "That's what partners do."

Partners. The word felt right, fitting, like a key sliding into a lock. But as I held her, I realized it wasn't enough.

Not anymore.

The room was quiet, the only sound the soft hum of the city below and the steady rhythm of her breathing. I could feel her heart beating against my chest, a steady, insistent pulse that matched the pounding in my own.

Slowly, I tilted her chin up with my free hand, her eyes meeting mine in the dim light. They were wide, searching, filled with questions she wasn't ready to voice. But I saw something else too, a hunger, a need that mirrored my own.

"Avery," I whispered, my voice rough with want.

She swallowed, her throat moving visibly beneath her skin. "Yes?"

I didn't answer with words. Instead, I leaned in, my lips brushing hers in a kiss that was soft, tentative, a question. She responded immediately, her lips parting beneath mine, her hands clutching at my shirt.

The kiss deepened, our mouths moving in sync, the taste of her, sweet and intoxicating, sending a jolt of desire straight to my core. I pulled her closer, my other hand sliding up her back, feeling the curve of her spine, the softness of her skin beneath the silk of her blouse.

She moaned softly, the sound vibrating against my lips, and I groaned in response, my control slipping as I pressed her back against the couch. Her legs parted, and I settled between them, our bodies aligned, the heat between us undeniable.

"God, Avery," I murmured against her neck, my lips trailing kisses along her jawline. "You have no idea what you do to me."

Her hands tangled in my hair, pulling me closer as she tilted her head back, exposing the delicate curve of her throat. "Show me," she breathed.

I didn't need to be told twice. My hands moved lower, sliding beneath her blouse, my fingers tracing the lace of her bra, the softness of her skin. She arched into my touch, her breath coming in short, sharp gasps as I unhooked her bra, baring her to my gaze.

Her breasts were perfect, full and round, her nipples tight peaks that begged to be touched. I leaned down, taking one into my mouth, my tongue swirling, my teeth grazing gently. She cried out, her hands tightening in my hair, her body trembling as I lavished attention on her, my hands roaming, my mouth devouring.

"Blake," she moaned, her voice thick with need. "Please."

I looked up, meeting her gaze, my heart pounding in my chest. "What do you want, Avery?"

Her eyes were dark, her lips swollen from my kisses. "You," she whispered. "I want you."

The words were like a match to gasoline. I stood, pulling her with me, her legs wrapping around my waist as I carried her to the bedroom. The house felt endless, the distance stretching on forever, but I didn't stop, couldn't stop, not with her in my arms, her lips pressed to my neck, her hands roaming, her body pressing against mine.

The bedroom was a blur of soft light and shadows, the bed a haven in the storm. I laid her down gently, my hands never leaving her body, my mouth never stopping its exploration. Her blouse was gone, her skirt pooled at her waist, and I followed, shedding my own clothes until we were both bare, our skin flushed, our desire palpable.

She was beautiful, her body a work of art, every curve, every line a temptation I couldn't resist. I knelt between her legs, my hands tracing the contours of her hips, my thumbs brushing the sensitive skin of her inner thighs.

She shivered, her eyes closing as she tilted her head back, offering herself to me completely.

"Blake," she whispered, her voice a plea.

I smiled, leaning down, my lips brushing her ear. "Tell me what you want."

Her eyes fluttered open, meeting mine, her breath coming in short, shallow gasps. "I want you inside me," she said, her voice steady despite the tremor in her body. "Now."

The demand sent a surge of heat through me, my body throbbing with need. I positioned myself at her entrance, teasing her with slow, deliberate strokes, watching her face as she bit her lip, her eyes closing in anticipation.

"Please," she whispered.

I thrust into her, filling her in one smooth motion, her walls tight and wet around me. She gasped, her head falling back, her hands gripping the sheets as I began to move, slow and steady at first, then harder, faster, our bodies moving in perfect rhythm.

The room was filled with the sounds of our passion, her moans, my groans, the slick rhythm of our bodies joining. I leaned over her, my hands bracing on either side of her head, my lips capturing hers in a kiss that was desperate, hungry, all-consuming.

"God, Avery," I murmured against her lips. "You feel so good."

She smiled, her hands sliding down my back, her nails digging into my skin. "Don't stop," she pleaded.

I didn't plan to. I moved faster, harder, our bodies slapping together, the friction building, the tension coiling tighter and tighter. Her legs wrapped around my waist, her heels digging into my ass, pulling me deeper, closer, until I was buried to the hilt.

"Blake," she cried, her voice breaking. "I'm close."

"Me too," I growled, my control slipping as I felt her walls tighten around me, her body trembling on the edge.

"Come with me," I urged, my voice hoarse. "Let go."

Her eyes met mine, her breath coming in short, sharp gasps. "Together," she whispered.

And then, we fell.

Her body shook as she climaxed, her cries filling the room, her walls milking me, drawing my own release. I groaned, my head falling to her shoulder as I emptied myself into her, our bodies joined, our hearts pounding in unison.

For a long moment, we lay there, entangled, our breaths slowly returning to normal, the world outside forgotten. I pulled out gently, rolling onto my back, Avery's head resting on my chest, her hand tracing lazy patterns on my stomach.

"That was..." she began, her voice trailing off.

"Yeah," I agreed, pressing a kiss to her forehead.

She smiled, her eyes closing as she snuggled closer. "We still have a leak to deal with."

I chuckled, wrapping my arms around her. "We do. But for now..."

She nodded, her breath evening out as sleep began to claim her. I held her, feeling the weight of the night, the promise of the morning, the knowledge that whatever came next, we'd face it together.

As her breathing deepened, I pressed a kiss to her hair, my heart full, my mind racing with the possibilities of what we'd done. The leak, the chaos, the world outside—it could wait. For now, there was only her and me, our bodies still humming with the aftermath of our passion, our hearts beating as one.

And as I drifted off to sleep, I knew one thing for certain: this was just the beginning.

The next morning, I found her in the kitchen, staring at the coffee maker as if willing it to work faster.

"You look like hell," I teased.

She shot me a dry look. "Thanks. Back at ya."

For a moment, it felt normal. Like we weren't in the middle of a war zone.

But then, Connor was at the door demanding entry. He walked in, his expression tense. "We have a problem."

"Do you ever have good news?" I complained, setting down my mug, "What kind of problem?"

Connor handed me a folder. "The usual kind."

I flipped it open, my stomach tightening as I read the contents. The weight of the past few weeks settled over me as I read the report he'd given me. Surveillance data. Financial transactions. A web of connections that didn't just tie back to Avery's company. It spread further. Wider.

I glanced at Avery. She was reading over my shoulder; her lips pressed into a tight line.

Connor folded his arms. "Ethan wasn't acting alone. And whoever's pulling the strings? They've been planning this for a long time."

My gut tightened. I had a bad feeling about this.

Avery took a slow breath. "So, what do we do now?"

I met her gaze. "We find out who the hell is behind this."

Chapter 17
Final Confrontation

Avery Lane

I had spent my life making calculated moves. But standing outside the abandoned processing plant, my heart pounding against my ribs, I felt anything but decided.

Blake stood beside me, his stance solid, his eyes scanning the perimeter. His presence was constant, steady, unwavering. I had come to depend on that strength more than I ever thought I could. I inhaled deeply. This was it.

"You don't have to do this," Blake murmured.

It was the second time he had brought it up. I knew why. He was trying to make sure I was safe, protected but this was my company, my life. I was damned well not sitting on the sidelines playing helpless damsel. They thought they could steamroll over me? Take everything I had created? Not in a million years. I would meet them face to face and end this once and for all.

I turned to him, lifting my chin. "Yes. I do."

His gaze held mine for a beat, then he nodded. No argument, no protest, just belief. That was why I trusted him. I adjusted the earpiece Connor had given me.

"Everyone in position?" Blake asked.

"Affirmative," Connor's voice crackled. "Eyes on target."

My fingers clenched around the small USB drive in my pocket. The final piece of the puzzle. The proof that the conspiracy extended beyond my company, beyond Ethan Graves. If we didn't stop this now, more than just my reputation would be at stake. The world was teetering on the edge tonight and only a few of us knew it. I was bound and determined to make sure tomorrow's sun rose on the same world it set on, whatever it took.

Blake shifted, his hand hovering near the gun at his side. "Move out."

We slipped inside through a service entrance, the scent of oil and rust thick in the air. My pulse quickened as I followed Blake through the dimly lit corridors, our footsteps nearly silent. The facility had been shut down for years, but it wasn't abandoned. Someone had repurposed it, crates of stolen tech, surveillance equipment, and boxed shipments lined the walls. I snarled seeing the name Lane Tech and my logo on a lot of them. Blake signaled for me to stop. He pressed a hand to my lower back, guiding me into a shadowed alcove.

"Three men ahead," he whispered. "Armed."

I exhaled slowly. We had talked about this. I wasn't the same woman who had denied that there were any real threats a few weeks ago. I knew the stakes, and everyone was playing for keeps tonight. Including me.

I met Blake's gaze. "We take them out quietly."

He had asked before what I was willing to do to protect what was mine. Tonight, it went beyond what was mine. Tonight, I was protecting the whole damn world.

A ghost of a smile touched his lips. "That's my girl."

Heat curled unexpectedly in my stomach, but there was no time to dwell on it. Blake moved first, a silent predator. I followed his lead, staying low, controlled. He struck fast. One guard dropped with a swift chokehold, another taken down before he could raise his weapon. The third barely had time to react before I swung a metal pipe, catching him across the jaw. He crumpled.

Blake turned to me, brow raised. "Nice work." He whispered.

I shrugged my shoulders. "I've been paying attention."

His smirk was short-lived as a sudden sound echoed through the space. Footsteps. More were coming.

My heart raced. "We need to move."

We pressed forward, navigating the maze of crates until we reached a large control room overlooking the warehouse floor. My stomach knotted at what I saw.

Below us, a group of men, loading high-end tech onto transport trucks. And in the center of them, orchestrating the chaos, Marcus Hale. My breath caught. The CEO of my biggest rival here in person. It had been him all along.

I turned to Blake, fury sparking in my veins as I hissed. "That's Marcus Hale, CEO of StarGroup. He's behind this. Not your friend Hale."

Blake's expression darkened. "Then let's end it."

We moved swiftly. Blake covered me as I accessed a terminal concealed by a stack of crates, plugging in the USB. If I could extract the data and send it to Connor, they would have the evidence needed to dismantle Hale's operation and prove he was behind it. A progress bar blinked on the screen.

Thirty percent.

A creak sounded behind us. Blake spun, gun raised. Too late.

A fist crashed into his ribs, sending him staggering. I barely had time to react before a hand clamped around my wrist, yanking me back. Marcus Hale smiled down at me.

"You just couldn't leave well enough alone, could you?"

I gritted my teeth. "You tried to ruin me."

Hale's grip tightened. "I did more than try."

I didn't think. I acted. Driving my knee up, I caught him in the gut. He cursed, releasing me, and I stumbled back, reaching for the nearest weapon, a keyboard. Blake had recovered, taking down another guard, but more were coming.

Seventy percent. Too slow!

I swung the keyboard two-handed as Hale lunged. The impact sent a sharp shock up my arms, but he barely flinched as it shattered. It gave Blake time to grab his collar, slamming him into the console.

"Give up." Blake growled.

Hale laughed, blood trickling from his lip. "You have no idea what you're up against."

The download completed. I grabbed the drive and stepped back. "I know enough."

Hale's smile didn't falter. "Do you?"

A screen flickered. A live feed. And my blood ran cold. It wasn't just about my company.

This was bigger.

My hands clenched around the USB drive as the live feed played out before me. Screens flickered, displaying a map with red markers spread across multiple cities: New York, London, Tokyo, more. Each pin represented a target. Each one tied back to Hale's company, StarGroup.

"He must be sending Vanguard out." I whispered.

"What will that do?" Blake demanded.

"It's every major bank and stock market. Think of it like the A-bomb of computer softwares that will lock down the entire world's financial markets into a nuclear meltdown overnight. Global catastrophe." I paled.

Blake's jaw tightened. "Can you stop it?"

Marcus Hale, bloodied but grinning, leaned against the console. "Took you long enough to figure it out but too late."

My pulse pounded in my ears. "What are you doing?"

Hale's smile widened. "Something much bigger than you, sweetheart."

Blake pressed his gun to Hale's temple. "Try again."

A flicker of something passed through Hale's eyes, but he chuckled. "Go ahead, Carter. Pull the trigger. It won't stop what's coming."

My grip on the USB tightened. "We have the evidence. You're done."

Hale licked the blood from his lip and simply shook his head.

"With my lawyers and what's going to hit? No one will even have time for me." Hale laughed.

A crackling sound filled the air. The monitors shifted, revealing lines of code running across the screens.

Blake cursed. "Something else activated."

My stomach twisted. I recognized the code. "It's an automated breach protocol."

Blake shot me a look. "In English."

My fingers flew over the keyboard. "It's a self-destruct sequence, for the data, for Vanguard. He's wiping everything from his trail."

Blake didn't hesitate. He turned and drove a fist into Hale's face, sending him sprawling. "Shut it down!"

I worked fast. My breath came in short bursts. I had to stop this. A final line of code. A beep. And then. The screens froze. The data remained intact.

I slumped back. "I stopped it."

Blake exhaled, turning to Hale. "Game over."

Hale groaned, lifting his head. His smirk was gone. "You think this ends with me?"

My stomach dropped.

Hale chuckled darkly. "You're playing in the big leagues now, Lane. And the people I answer to? They won't let this slide."

Blake's expression darkened. "Who?"

Hale's smile was chilling. "You'll find out soon enough."

Chapter 18
Love in the Line of Fire
Blake Connor

The weight of my Glock felt like an extension of my arm as I swept through the darkened corridors of the Avery's tech lab. She moved beside me, her breath steady, her mind as sharp as the algorithms that had built her empire. We had one shot at this. She had to take down the network in order to neutralize the Vanguard threat. Then we just had to make it out alive. Yeah. Simple.

We had thought we were home free at the warehouse. We should have known better. While I dealt with the police and the mopping up operation, Avery had sat down at the terminal to make sure Vanguard and the world was safe. When I was finished, I had thoughts of a very intimate evening at her penthouse by way of celebration.

I did until I saw her pinched face staring at the monitors as she typed on multiple keyboards, accessing things faster than I could follow. Turned out, Vanguard and the world were not safe. Hale's threats were real. Someone higher up the food chain was copying Vanguard into their own network and proceeding with the plan. The only way to stop them was to get to the lab and for Avery to install a lock keyed to her own bio-imprint. As she explained it, it was like the ultimate gun safe. Without her personal retina and handprint, no one would be able to access Vanguard. So, here we were. Of course, whoever had gotten here before us simply to prevent us from doing exactly what we were trying to do. They'd been steps ahead of us this whole damn time.

Avery was trying to stop a cyberwar that could level the global economy. Her ex, her competitive rival, her CFO and some other higher player were leveraging Vanguard's AI into a ransomware weapon, planning to hold global banks hostage and shut down the exchange markets while playing god with the financial systems. That ended tonight, one way or another. If Avery wasn't a tech genius in her own right, we'd all be eating MREs and boiling water come tomorrow but I had faith. As long as I could get her to the mainframe inside this lab.

"Clear left," I murmured, signaling Avery forward. The air crackled with tension, the faint hum of servers whirring around us.

"We need to get to the central server room," Avery whispered, her voice as calm as if we weren't seconds from potential death and worldwide catastrophe. "Everything runs through that hub. If I can inject my kill code—"

A noise from up ahead. I spun, pressing Avery against the wall, shielding her with my body as footsteps echoed from the next corridor. My earpiece crackled.

"Two coming your way," came the voice of Connor, from the van outside watching a heat seeking drone. "Armed. Moving fast."

The regular lab security were now just bodies in the halls. I didn't check but I doubted any were still breathing. The guys we were facing weren't in it for a few lousy billion. They were playing for world domination. A few security guys trying to hold the lab didn't stand a chance.

Avery had gone pale at the sight of the first of her employees in a pool of blood. Then she had tightened her jaw and looked like she wanted to kill anyone who got in her way. I was starting to love this woman. Maybe the correct term was 'love even more'.

"Copy," I whispered. I turned to Avery, holding her gaze for a split second longer than necessary. "Stay behind me."

She didn't argue. We had gotten to a point of mutual respect. She knew I was going to get in front of her when things went sideways and not just because it was my job. I was better at these kinds of things. And I knew not to argue about her coming inside. She was the one who had to stop this. Hoping I could neutralize all the threats and then go out to bring her in to a terminal wasn't realistic. The odds were stacked against us. We needed to get to the mainframe where she could work while I held off whoever was coming after us and we had to do it as fast as possible. After that? I could only hope we made it back out. It was a thin hope. At least we were together.

The moment the guards rounded the corner, I moved. Two shots, silenced, dropped them before they even registered my threat. I grabbed one of their keycards not even bothering to check for a pulse. They'd been center of mass kill shots. I wasn't messing around. Avery's eyes flicked to mine, unspoken words passing between us. She understood we were not here to take prisoners. We were trying to save the friggin world.

"You good?" I asked.

We hadn't talked about how far things might go tonight. I figured the stakes in this endgame pretty much spelled it out, but I needed her to be ready to do her part. Her eyes showed the whites, but she swallowed, nodded and kept her focus away from the bodies.

"Never better. Let's go." She said quietly.

We didn't encounter anyone else in the quiet halls. The server room was a fortress, reinforced steel doors, keycard locks, an entire security system designed to keep out intruders. But Avery was no ordinary intruder. This was her world.

"I need thirty seconds once we're in," she murmured, already pulling a small drive from her pocket. "If I can override their encryption, I can shut it all down and put in my lock."

"Make it twenty," I said, getting a report of more guards from Connor.

We moved fast. I swiped the stolen keycard, Avery's fingers flew over the keypad, and the door hissed open. I stepped in first, sweeping the room, my heart hammering against my ribs. Clear.

Avery darted to the main console, plugging in her drive. "I'm in."

Then an alarm blared through the empty halls.

"Shit," I muttered, spinning toward the door. Some security override. They knew where we were.

Avery cursed under her breath. "I need a minute."

"We don't have a minute," I growled, taking position by the entrance, my gun raised.

Heavy boots pounded down the hallway. My earpiece crackled. "Blake, you've got company. Four, maybe five," Connor warned.

I exhaled, centering myself. "Make that my problem. Just get the job done, Avery."

The first man burst around the corner of the hall, rifle in his hand. I fired first, dropping him. Another came in low from a cross hall, forcing me into hand-to-hand. His fist clipped my ribs right where I'd been knifed, but I drove an elbow into his throat, sending him staggering. A third attacker lunged, too close to shoot. I used his momentum against him, slamming him into the server racks with a sickening crunch.

Behind me, Avery shouted frantically. "Almost there!"

The fourth attacker fired blindly into the room. A bullet grazed my arm. I gritted my teeth, took cover, and returned fire. He dropped.

"Shut down. Installing lock." Avery yelled.

The servers flickered. The ransomware attack was stopped cold. I took a full breath. Too soon. The fight wasn't over.

Warren Merrick, the damned chairman of the board, stood in the doorway, a gun aimed squarely at Avery's chest.

"Drop it or do you want me to demonstrate my marksman titles?" he ordered.

I clenched my jaw. My finger hovered over the trigger, but Avery was in the line of fire.

"Blake," she murmured, her voice steady despite the gun aimed at her head.

"Let her go," I said. My voice was a lethal promise.

The Chairman smirked. "Do you even know what you're protecting, Connor? She's a liability. A weakness." He stepped into the room to press the barrel against Avery's skull. "One I have used."

Avery's fingers twitched slightly, just enough for me to understand. A signal. She had a plan. At least I prayed that's what she was telling me. I took the risk. In one motion, I dropped to a crouch, fired a single shot, straight through his wrist. The gun clattered to the floor. Avery spun, driving her elbow into his ribs before kicking him backward. I moved fast, pressing my boot to his chest as I aimed my Glock between his eyes.

"I have always wanted to say make my day, asshole," I said.

His eyes darkened with something close to admiration. "You don't have the guts."

"I do." Avery spat out in fury, holding out her hand.

I considered it. I really, truly did. This man had tried to kill Avery, the woman who had come to mean so much to me. But in the end, I wasn't an executioner. I holstered my weapon.

"Connor, send in the cleanup team," I said into my comm.

The Chairman smirked, but it faded when I turned to Avery.

"You good?" I asked, brushing my fingers over her cheek.

She exhaled shakily. "I am now."

The moment stretched, the air charged with the weight of what had just happened. The Chairman groaned beneath my boot, his fingers twitching toward his wounded wrist.

"Give me an excuse," I warned, "Please."

His sneer remained, but his fight was gone. Outside, the wail of approaching sirens signaled the end of his reign.

Avery took a shaky breath. "Lock installed. It's over."

Almost. I grabbed a zip tie from my belt and secured the Chairman's hands behind his back. "You planned this from the start, didn't you?" I asked, tightening the binds.

His smirk widened. "You really think you won? That taking me down ends this?" His voice dripped with contempt. "I'm not alone. There are others. This isn't over."

Avery stepped closer, her gaze unwavering. "It is for you. And I'm forewarned and trust me, I am more dangerous than you can imagine."

The hallway was suddenly flooded with tactical officers led by Connor, his rifle raised.

"Jesus, Connor," I muttered, shaking my head as I took in the scene. "You sure know how to make an entrance."

I stepped back as they took the Chairman into custody. My job was done. Or at least, it should have been. Avery's gaze met mine. The reality of what we'd just been through hit hard. The adrenaline that had kept me sharp was starting to fade, leaving behind exhaustion and something deeper. Something I hadn't let myself feel in a long time.

Relief.

Avery's fingers brushed my arm, her touch grounding me. "You okay?"

I huffed a breath, running a hand through my sweat-dampened hair. "You're the one who had a gun to her head, Lane. Shouldn't I be asking you that?"

She let out a soft laugh, but there was something raw behind it. "I knew you'd find a way."

That trust, that belief, it did something to me. I liked it. Probably more than I should.

I swallowed hard. "You should probably get checked out. Make sure—"

"I'm fine," she interrupted, but there was a slight tremor in her voice.

I didn't argue. Instead, I reached for her hand. She let me. The team finished securing the scene, the Chairman and his remaining men loaded into the waiting convoy. As the chaos settled, I found myself standing outside the facility, the cool night air hitting my overheated skin. Avery stood beside me, arms wrapped around herself.

"You did good in there," I said. "You know, you saved the whole damn world tonight and no one will ever know it."

She glanced at me, something unreadable in her eyes. "So did you."

Silence stretched, but it wasn't uncomfortable. It was charged with everything we hadn't said. Everything we couldn't ignore anymore.

I exhaled sharply. "Avery..."

She turned to me fully, her expression softening. "Blake, I—"

I didn't let her finish. I closed the distance between us, capturing her lips with mine. She gasped against my mouth before melting into me, her hands clutching my shirt like she was afraid to let go. And maybe I was, too. The kiss was desperate, a culmination of every moment that had led us here. Of every argument, every stolen glance, every second I'd fought what I felt. When we finally broke apart, our breaths mingled in the night air.

Avery rested her forehead against mine. "What now?"

I swallowed. That was the question, wasn't it? For the first time, I didn't have an answer.

Avery's grip on my shirt tightened. "Blake," she whispered. "I know I don't need a bodyguard now, but I don't want this to be over."

Neither did I. My fingers traced her arm. She had been strong, but I could see it now, the weight of everything catching up to her.

I cupped her face, my thumb brushing her cheek. "It's not," I murmured. "Not if you don't want it to be."

She searched my face, deciding if she could believe me. I'd spent too long pretending this was just a job. But it never was. The world shrank to just the two of us.

"I don't know how this works," she admitted.

"Me neither," I confessed.

Her lips parted into a gentle smile. "Then we figure it out. Together."

I nodded. The fight was over. But what came next?

Chapter 19
Promise of a New Beginning
Avery Lane

The morning light filtered through the floor-to-ceiling windows of my penthouse, casting golden streaks over the hardwood floor. The city below pulsed with life, oblivious to the chaos that had nearly consumed the world.

For the first time in weeks, I felt safe.

Blake stood by the window, arms crossed, his profile carved in quiet strength. The bruises on his jaw had darkened overnight, a stark reminder of what we'd endured. But he was here. We both were. And that was enough.

He turned, catching me watching him. A slow smirk curved his lips. "Thinking about how great I look in your apartment?"

I huffed a laugh, rolling onto my side. "Maybe. You do make a pretty good bodyguard, when you're not pissing me off."

Blake chuckled, walking over to sit on the edge of the bed. The mattress dipped beneath his weight. He reached out, brushing a strand of hair from my face. The gesture was gentle, so at odds with the hardened soldier he tried to be.

"What happens now?" I murmured.

His expression turned serious. "That depends on you, Lane."

The weight of his words settled between us. For so long, my life had been dictated by schedules, acquisitions, and relentless ambition. Everything had been about building, expanding, controlling. But now, everything felt different. I propped myself up on one elbow, searching his face.

"I need to rebuild. My company. My reputation. Vanguard. Everything."

Blake nodded. "I figured."

"But I don't want to do it alone," I admitted. The words felt foreign, but right. Vulnerability had never come easy to me, but with Blake, it wasn't weakness. It was truth.

His brow arched. "Are you asking me to be your business partner, Lane?"

I smirked. "Would you say yes?"

He considered it for a moment, then shook his head. "Nah. I hate boardrooms. Too many suits."

I laughed. "Okay, fair. But you could stick around." My voice softened. "Stay with me."

Blake exhaled, running a hand through his hair. "I won't lie to you, Avery. This is new for me. The whole... sticking around thing."

I reached for his hand. "Then we figure it out together."

He didn't answer right away, but he didn't pull away either. And that was enough for now.

The next few days passed in a blur of damage control. Lawyers. PR statements. Meetings with my board. Having to let so many people go. The fallout from all the arrests sent shockwaves through the industry, and while my company had been targeted, it had survived. Barely. Through it all, Blake stayed close. He wasn't my shadow now, but I'd catch glimpses of him, lingering near the elevators, standing in the background at press events, keeping an eye on me without being overbearing. It was comforting in a way I hadn't expected. One evening, after a particularly grueling meeting, I found him in my office, boots propped up on my desk. He was back in his trademark brown leather jacket, black t-shirt and jeans. Now, it just seemed totally natural on him. Definitely not a pizza delivery guy.

"You know, most people don't put their feet on other people's desks," I teased, closing the door behind me.

Blake smirked. "I'm not most people."

I walked over, perching on the desk beside him. "No, you are not." I swore with an appreciative grin.

He studied me for a long moment before speaking. "You're handling this." It wasn't a question. It was a statement of fact.

I exhaled, rubbing my temples. "Barely."

"You're stronger than you think, Lane."

I met his gaze. "So are you." Something shifted between us then. An understanding. A promise.

A week later, Blake surprised me. "Pack a bag," he said, tossing a duffel onto my bed.

I blinked at him. "Excuse me?"

"We're getting out of here."

I frowned. "Blake, I can't just—"

"Yes, you can," he interrupted. "You need to."

I hesitated. My instinct was to argue, to say there was too much work, too much at stake. But when I looked at him, I realized he was right. I'd spent so much time fighting, surviving, starting the rebuilding. But I hadn't taken a second to breathe. So, I listened. We ended up in a secluded cabin by a quiet lake, miles away from the city. The air was crisp, the silence soothing. I hadn't felt this at peace in years. Blake, ever the soldier, checked the perimeter before relaxing. When he finally sat beside me on the porch, the sunset painting the sky in hues of gold and violet, I reached for his hand.

"Thank you," I murmured.

"For what?"

"For reminding me that there's more to life than fighting."

He squeezed my hand. "I'm just glad you finally listened."

The cabin felt like a world away from everything we had endured. No boardrooms, no security briefings, no looming threats. Just us. That first night, we sat on the wooden deck, wrapped in blankets, watching the fire crackle in the stone pit. The stars above were endless, stretching across the sky in a way that made me feel small, but in a good way. I didn't need to run the universe or save it. I was just a part of it.

Blake took a slow sip of his beer, his free hand still resting in mine. "You ever do this?" he asked.

I glanced at him. "What? Sit outside and stare at the stars?"

"Yeah. Just... exist."

I exhaled softly. "Not really. My life has always been about what's next. The next program. The next launch. The next deal. The next crisis."

Blake was quiet for a moment, then said, "You don't have to live like that anymore."

I turned to him, searching his face. "What about you?"

He shrugged. "I spent my whole life waiting for the next deployment. The next mission. I never thought about what came after."

"And now?"

Blake laced his fingers through mine. "Now I have a reason to." The air between us thickened, charged with something deeper than words.

I set my drink down, shifting to face him fully. "Blake, I—" He silenced me with a kiss. It wasn't rushed or desperate, like the kisses we had stolen in the heat of danger. This was different, unhurried, certain. A promise in itself.

When we pulled apart, his forehead rested against mine. "I'm all in, Lane."

I swallowed against the lump in my throat. "Me too."

The fire crackled beside us, but I barely noticed. My entire world had narrowed to the man in front of me. For the first time in as long as I could remember, I wasn't thinking about the past or worrying about the future. I was here. With him. And it was enough.

The rest of our time at the cabin passed in a blissful blur. Lazy mornings wrapped in each other's arms. Afternoons spent hiking through the woods, our conversations drifting between deep confessions and playful teasing. Evenings where we cooked together, well, where Blake cooked, and I attempted to help. By the time we packed up to leave, a new certainty had settled between us.

As we drove back toward the city, the skyline looming in the distance, I glanced at Blake. "What happens now?" I asked.

He smirked, keeping his eyes on the road. "We face it together."

And for the first time, that didn't scare me. It felt like home.

Back in the city, life moved fast again, but this time, it felt different. The weight of responsibility hadn't vanished, but it no longer felt like it would crush me. Blake stayed. He didn't say it outright, didn't make some grand declaration, but I knew it in the way he never strayed too far, how he showed up at my office with coffee, how he looked at me when he thought I wasn't paying attention.

We fell into a rhythm. Days filled with meetings and decisions, nights spent curled together in my apartment, tangled in sheets and whispered words. One evening, as we sat on my balcony overlooking the city, he stretched his legs out, propping them on the railing. "So, what's next for Avery Lane?"

I exhaled, considering my answer. "Rebuilding. Expanding. But on my terms this time."

Blake turned his head to me, studying me. "And what about us?"

I smiled, reaching for his hand. "That's the easiest answer of all."

He raised a brow. "Yeah?"

"Yeah," I said softly. "We figure it out together."

He squeezed my hand. "Damn right, we do."

And just like that, the future didn't feel so uncertain anymore.

Blake stayed beside me as the days turned into weeks. He still had his own life, his own work, but he always found his way back to me. And I let him in, little by little, realizing that love wasn't something that had to be fought for. It was something that was simply given.

One night, as we lay in bed, his arm draped over my waist, he murmured, "You're stuck with me now, Lane."

I smiled into the darkness. "Good."

Because for the first time, I wasn't afraid of what came next. I was ready for it.

Want to join Jax' Inner Circle?

Every Jax Kane book has a secret code word at the end.

Collect them to unlock sneak peeks, bonus chapters, and early cover reveals.

Your secret code word for *Protecting the Grumpy CEO* is: **TECHNOLOGY**.

Enter it here to start your collection:

https://forms.gle/JTGzCbssuofe3HTp8

A Few Final Words From Jax

Hi, Jax Friend!

I hope you enjoyed reading *Protecting the Grumpy CEO* as much as I enjoyed writing it!

Did you know that reader reviews are largely what determine how books get ranked when someone searches on Amazon?

It is **vitally** important for indie creators, like me, to get reviews from people like you.

So, please consider heading over to Amazon and giving this book an honest sentence or two review. You can just look up the book: *Protecting the Grumpy CEO* by Jax Kane. OR click the link https://amzn.to/4niq33f

And if you liked this Sierra Bravo Security adventure, there are more for you to read!

Locked Down with the Bodyguard: A party girl finds herself the target of a cartel. One tough ex-Marine bodyguard to the rescue! They're stuck in a mountain cabin all by themselves. Uh-oh. Passion and gunshots soon follow! https://amzn.to/4pkBlWL

Or, *Stuck with my Ex's Brother*: They survive a plane crash but a killer is on the loose. The bodyguard and the nurse run – on a mountain, in a blizzard, pursued by the killer, hoping to get somewhere to call for help. https://amzn.to/4ozKCsP

Follow me on my Amazon author page to get 1st notice about my new releases! Another new Sierra Bravo Security story is coming soon! A pop star is being stalked and needs a great bodyguard. Sierra Bravo's got a full line-up! Here's the address for my author page so you don't miss that one: www.amazon.com/author/jaxkane and an easy link https://www.amazon.com/author/jaxkane

And if you haven't read the first book in the Sierra Bravo Security series, *Pretending with the Protector*, you can get it here for **FREE** https://dl.bookfunnel.com/ono7q131mr

Thanks for reading! Readers mean the world to me.

Your friend,

Jax

Printed in Dunstable, United Kingdom